A Room

E.M. FORSTER

Level 6

Retold by Hilary Maxwell-Hyslop
Series Editors: Andy Hopkins and Jocelyn Potter

Pearson Education Limited
Edinburgh Gate, Harlow,
Essex CM20 2JE, England
and Associated Companies throughout the world.

ISBN: 978-1-4058-6530-2

First published by Edward Arnold 1908
First published by Penguin Books 2003
This edition first published 2008

3 5 7 9 10 8 6 4 2

Typeset by Graphicraft Ltd, Hong Kong
Set in 11/14pt Bembo
Printed in China
SWTC/01

Published by Pearson Education Ltd in association with
Penguin Books Ltd, both companies being subsidiaries of Pearson Plc

For a complete list of the titles available in the Penguin Readers series please write to your local
Pearson Longman office or to: Penguin Readers Marketing Department, Pearson Education,
Edinburgh Gate, Harlow, Essex CM20 2JE, England.

Contents

Introduction

'You can change love, ignore it, muddle it, but you can never pull it out of you. The poets are right. Love lasts for ever.'

A Room with a View is set at the beginning of the twentieth century. Lucy Honeychurch is a young English woman on holiday in Italy with her older cousin, Charlotte Bartlett, who is acting as her chaperone. They are staying in Florence at an Italian pension for British guests, but are disappointed with the poor view from their windows. While they are discussing their misfortune, they are interrupted by a guest at another table, an Englishman called Mr Emerson, who has heard their conversation. He and his son, George, are both in rooms that offer beautiful views of Florence, but Mr Emerson offers to exchange rooms with the two unhappy ladies. At first, Charlotte refuses. This is partly because she does not want to accept a favour from anybody, but it is also because Mr Emerson and his son come from a lower social background. Eventually, however, she changes her mind about Mr Emerson's offer.

Over the next few days, Lucy develops a strange liking for the Emersons, who are considered socially unacceptable by the other guests. After a number of adventures, Lucy realises with horror that George is in love with her. But even more worrying and confusing for her is the fact that she feels mysteriously attracted to him. Lucy returns to England and her familiar world of tennis and tea parties. She becomes engaged to the intellectual, socially well-connected Cecil Vyse, which pleases her mother. But her experience in Italy has changed her. It has opened doors to new possibilities, and somewhere deep inside her she cannot forget George Emerson...

A Room with a View, by E.M. Forster, gives us a clear picture of middle-class life in England at the beginning of the twentieth century. We can see the importance that was given to social position and proper behaviour. Forster's careful observation of the attitudes and behaviour of the English is sometimes humorous but never cruel. He understands the influences on his characters and the motives for their actions; even Charlotte Bartlett and Cecil Vyse, whose behaviour often seems ridiculous, are treated sympathetically.

A Room with a View is Forster's most romantic, optimistic book. Like his other novels, it deals with the problem of people attempting to communicate with and understand each other across social barriers. On the one side are the traditional people, who accept the standard values of society and do not want anything to change. Forster often used to refer to these people as his 'flat' characters. Their attitudes and behaviour remain constant as the story develops, and they (Miss Bartlett, Cecil Vyse, Mrs Honeychurch) are often the source of humour. On the other side are people whose ideas and attitudes change as the story develops. Forster referred to these (Lucy, the Emersons, Freddy) as his 'round' characters. In *A Room with a View*, the 'round' characters are more unconventional. They are constantly asking questions, trying to change things, while the more conventional 'flat' characters try to stop them.

Lucy represents the type of young person who was growing up in England at the beginning of the twentieth century. She is bright and talented, but is not yet confident enough to challenge or question the attitudes of the people around her. Italy, however, changes her, and creates in her a desire to experience the world outside the narrowness of her own society.

Somewhere between the 'flat' and 'round' people lies the interesting, humorous character of Mr Beebe. Although he is a clergyman, he is a realist and is less threatened by unconventional ideas and behaviour than the others. He is impressed by the raw emotion of Lucy's piano-playing, he is the only person at the pension who is friendly to the Emersons, and he clearly has little respect for narrow-minded people like Miss Bartlett. However, he is not at heart a true rebel; he simply enjoys being naughtily playful. He likes seeing the discomfort of the 'flat' people, but loses interest in 'round' people when they develop too much and move outside his power to influence.

An important feature of the story is Forster's use of 'rooms' and 'views' as symbols of conventional and unconventional attitudes. Uncreative, traditional characters like Mrs Honeychurch and Cecil Vyse are often shown inside rooms. More unconventional characters like Freddy and the Emersons are often described as being outside. This represents their greater open-mindedness and imagination. At the beginning of the story, we learn a lot about the contrast between Miss Bartlett, Lucy and the Emersons from their differing attitudes towards the importance of having a 'room with a view'. Miss Bartlett wants a room with a good view, but shows little enthusiasm for exploring the city. Lucy is happy to have a room with a good view because this encourages her to explore the city itself, which leads to her adventures with George. The Emersons are happy to exchange rooms because they are more interested in discovering the city for themselves than in looking at it from a window.

A Room with a View is not, however, only a record of a way of life that disappeared many years ago. It is also a love story. The idea of forbidden love was very close to Forster's own heart. He himself was sexually attracted to men, but he never made this public during his lifetime. Instead, he wrote frequently about people's secret search for true love. In *A Room with a View*, Lucy's desire for George must remain a secret, even from herself, because the society she belongs to would never accept it. In a similar way, Forster had to hide his true feelings of love for men from a society that would never have understood or accepted them.

The placing of the first part of the story in Italy is significant. For Forster, as for many other people at that time, Italy was a place of freedom and sexual expression. Italy offered an atmosphere where raw passion was a possibility, unlike the narrow-mindedness of traditional English society. Lucy's experiences in Italy completely change her view of the world. She would never, for example, have been kissed by a boy who worked on the railways or witnessed a murder in a public square if she had stayed in the small, safe, protected world of Windy Corner. Without these experiences, her development as a human being might never have begun, and she would never have discovered the road to true happiness.

Edward Morgan Forster was born in 1879 into Victorian England, a world without cars, aeroplanes or television. He lived through a period of enormous social change, and died in 1970, the same year that the Beatles split up. He was an only child, and his father was an architect who died when Forster was a year old. He went to school in Kent and to Cambridge University, after which he travelled around Europe with his mother. He continued to live with his mother in Surrey until her death in 1945. He travelled widely during his lifetime, including visits to Italy, Greece, Germany and India, and he used his observations of the English abroad in his novels. During the winter of 1916–17, he met and fell in love with a seventeen-year-old boy in Alexandria, Egypt, and was heartbroken when the young man died of a serious illness in 1922. He worked in India in the early 1920s, and wrote his most successful novel, *A Passage to India*, after his return. *A Passage to India* was the last of his novels to be published during his lifetime.

After 1924, Forster wrote very little fiction apart from short stories intended only for himself and a small circle of friends. He did not, however, stop writing completely. He wrote a couple of plays, the story for a film (*A Diary for Timothy*, 1945) and, in 1951, the words for *Billy Budd*, an opera by his friend Benjamin Britten. People disagree about why Forster stopped writing novels, but it is thought that the world was changing too quickly for him. The world that he was familiar with had disappeared, and he did not understand the new world enough to write about it.

In the 1930s and 40s, Forster became a successful broadcaster on BBC radio. After the death of his mother, he accepted an academic position at King's College, Cambridge. In 1960, he was called as a witness for the defence in the trial of the publishers of a famous novel by D.H. Lawrence, *Lady Chatterley's Lover*, which was facing a ban. The publishers won the case.

Forster had five novels published in his lifetime: *Where Angels Fear to Tread* (1905), *The Longest Journey* (1907), *A Room with a View* (1908), *Howards End* (1910) and *A Passage to India* (1924). A sixth novel, *Maurice*, was not published until 1971, a year after his death. A seventh novel, *Arctic Summer*, remained unfinished.

A Room with a View may paint an interesting picture of a world that disappeared many years ago, but its emotional drama is still very powerful. Lucy's struggle to make sense of her feelings towards the two very different men in her life is as relevant now as it was a century ago. The director James Ivory made a famous film of the story for the cinema in 1986.

PART ONE The English in Italy

Chapter 1 The Pension Bertolini

'The *Signora*★ should not have done it,' said Miss Charlotte Bartlett. 'She should not have done it at all. She promised us south rooms with a view, close together. Instead, we are in north rooms, facing inwards and a long way apart. Oh, Lucy!'

'And she comes from London!' said her young cousin, Miss Lucy Honeychurch, who had been disappointed by the accent of the pension's owner. She looked at the two rows of English people who were sitting at the table; at the row of white bottles of water and red bottles of wine; at the pictures of royalty and a famous poet that hung in heavy frames on the wall. 'Charlotte, don't you feel that we might be in London, not Florence? I can hardly believe that all kinds of other things are just outside. I suppose it's because I'm so tired. I wanted so much to see the Arno. The rooms the Signora promised us in her letter would have looked over the river. She should not have done it. Oh, it is a shame!'

'Any little room is all right for me,' Miss Bartlett said, 'but it does seem hard that you shouldn't have a view.'

Lucy felt that she had been selfish. 'Charlotte, you mustn't spoil me; of course, you must look over the Arno too. I meant that. The first vacant room in the front – '

'You must have it,' said Miss Bartlett, part of whose travelling expenses were paid by Lucy's mother. Miss Bartlett frequently referred to this generosity.

'No, no. *You* must have it.'

'I insist on it. Your mother would never forgive me, Lucy.'

'She would never forgive *me*.'

★*Signora*: the Italian title for a woman; Mrs or madam

1

The two ladies' voices grew louder – and in fact a little cross. They were tired, and wanting to appear unselfish, they argued. Some of the other guests looked at each other, and one of them leant forward over the table and actually interrupted their argument.

'I have a view,' he said. 'My room has a view.'

Miss Bartlett was surprised. She knew the man was not from a similar social background, even before she glanced at him. He was an old man, of heavy build, with a fair, shaven face and large eyes. There was something childish in those eyes, though it was not the childishness of extreme old age.

'This is my son,' said the old man. 'His name's George. He has a view too.'

'Ah,' said Miss Bartlett, stopping Lucy, who was going to speak.

'What I mean,' he continued, 'is that you can have our rooms, and we'll have yours. We'll change.'

The better class of tourist was shocked at this, and sympathetic to the newcomers.

Miss Bartlett, in reply, said, 'Thank you very much indeed; that is impossible.'

'Why?' said the old man, with both fists on the table.

'Because it is quite impossible, thank you.'

'You see, we don't like to take – ' began Lucy.

Her cousin again stopped her.

'But why?' the old man repeated. 'Women like looking at a view, men don't.' And he turned to his son, saying, 'George, persuade them!'

'It's so obvious they should have the rooms,' said the son. 'There's nothing else to say.'

He did not look at the ladies as he spoke, but his voice was puzzled and sorrowful. Lucy, too, was puzzled, but she saw that there was going to be a problem. The old man went on asking Miss Bartlett why she would not change. He and his son would move out of their rooms in half an hour.

Miss Bartlett was powerless to deal with such insistence. Her face went red with displeasure and she looked around at the others. Two little old ladies looked back, seeming to say, 'We are not like him; we know how to behave.'

'Eat your dinner, dear,' she said to Lucy.

Lucy whispered that the father and son seemed very odd.

'Eat your dinner, dear. This pension is a failure. Tomorrow we will make a change.'

Miss Bartlett had hardly announced this decision, when she changed her mind. The curtains at the end of the room parted and revealed a clergyman, large but attractive, who hurried forward to take his place at the table, cheerfully apologising for his lateness.

Lucy at once got up, crying, 'Oh, oh! It's Mr Beebe! Oh, how perfectly lovely! Oh Charlotte, we must stay now, however bad the rooms are. Oh!'

Miss Bartlett said, with more control, 'How do you do, Mr Beebe? I expect that you have forgotten us: Miss Bartlett and Miss Honeychurch, who were at Tunbridge Wells when you helped the vicar of St Peter's Church that very cold Easter.'

The clergyman, who looked like someone on holiday, did not remember the ladies quite as well as they remembered him. But he came forward pleasantly, and accepted the chair which Lucy offered him.

'I *am* so glad to see you,' said the girl, who would have been glad to talk to the waiter if her cousin Charlotte Bartlett had given her permission. 'Isn't it funny how small the world is. And now there is Summer Street, too.'

'Miss Honeychurch lives in the parish of Summer Street,' said Miss Bartlett, 'and she mentioned that you have just agreed to go there as the vicar – '

'Quite right,' said Mr Beebe. 'I move into the vicarage at Summer Street next June. I am lucky to be going to such a charming neighbourhood.'

'Oh, how glad I am! The name of our house is Windy Corner,' said Lucy. 'There is Mother and me usually, and my brother, Freddy, though we don't often get him to ch . . . the church is rather far away, I mean.'

'Lucy dearest, let Mr Beebe eat his dinner.'

'I am eating it, thank you, and enjoying it,' said Mr Beebe.

He preferred to talk to Lucy, whose piano-playing he remembered, rather than to Miss Bartlett, who probably remembered his sermons. He asked the girl whether she knew Florence well, and was informed that she had never been there before. It is delightful to advise a newcomer, and he was the first to do so.

'Don't ignore the country around Florence,' he told her finally. 'On the first fine afternoon, drive up to Fiesole.'*

'No!' cried a voice from the top of the table. 'Mr Beebe, you are wrong. The first fine afternoon, your ladies must go to Prato. That place is both charming *and* dirty. I love it.'

'That lady looks so clever,' whispered Miss Bartlett to her cousin. 'We are in luck.'

And they were, in fact, flooded with information and advice. The other guests had decided, almost enthusiastically, that they were suitable, and had accepted them.

The young man named George glanced at the clever lady, and then returned silently to his food. Obviously he and his father were not considered suitable. Lucy wished that they were. She did not like the fact that they were excluded, and as she rose to go, she gave the two outsiders a nervous little bow.

The father did not see it. The son smiled back at her.

Lucy hurried after her cousin, who had already gone to the next room, and was sitting talking to Mr Beebe.

'We are most grateful to you,' she was saying. 'The first evening is so important. When you arrived, we were having a

*Fiesole, Prato: two towns near Florence

4

very difficult fifteen minutes. Do you, by any chance, know the name of the old man who sat opposite us at dinner?'

'Emerson.'

'Is he a friend of yours?'

'We are friendly – as one is in pensions.'

'Then I will say no more.'

He encouraged her a little, and she said more.

'I am the chaperone of my young cousin, Lucy, and it would be very serious if I put her under an obligation to people whom we did not know. His manner was not very polite. I hope I did the right thing.'

'Your reaction is quite understandable,' he said. He seemed thoughtful, and after a few moments added, 'But I don't think there would be much harm if you accepted.'

'No *harm*, of course. But we could not be under an obligation.'

'He is rather a peculiar man.' Again Mr Beebe hesitated, and then said gently, 'I think he would not take advantage of you, nor expect you to show your gratitude. He is someone who says exactly what he means. He has rooms he does not value, and he thinks you would value them.'

Lucy was pleased and said, 'I was hoping that he was nice. I always hope that people will be nice.'

'I think he is; nice but awkward. I disagree with him about almost everything important. But he is the sort of person that one disagrees with rather than disapproves of. When he first came here, he upset people. He is not tactful, and his manners are not good, and he always expresses his opinions. We nearly complained about him, but I am pleased to say that in the end we decided not to.'

'Should I assume that he is a Socialist?' asked Miss Bartlett.

Mr Beebe accepted this assessment, trying not to smile.

'And I presume he has brought his son up to be a Socialist as well?'

'I hardly know George, but he seems a nice person. He is like his father, so it is possible that he, too, may be a Socialist.'

'So you think I ought to have accepted their offer? You think I have been too suspicious?'

'Not at all,' he answered. 'I never suggested that.'

'But shouldn't I apologise for my apparent rudeness?'

He replied, a little annoyed, that it would be quite unnecessary, and left for the smoking room.

'Was I a bore?' said Miss Bartlett, as soon as he had disappeared. 'Why didn't you talk, Lucy? He prefers young people, I'm sure.'

'He is nice,' said Lucy. 'Just what I remember. He seems to see good in everyone. And you know how clergymen generally laugh. Mr Beebe laughs just like an ordinary man.'

'Funny girl! You remind me of your mother. I wonder if she will approve of Mr Beebe.'

'I'm sure she will; and so will Freddy.'

'I think everyone at Windy Corner will approve; it is the fashionable world. I am used to Tunbridge Wells, where we are still living in the past. I am afraid you are finding me a very sad companion.'

Lucy thought, 'I must have been selfish or unkind. I must be more careful. It is so awful for Charlotte, being poor.'

Fortunately, one of the little old ladies joined them, and asked if she could sit where Mr Beebe had sat. She began to chat gently about Italy, then sighed. 'If only Mr Emerson was more tactful. We were so sorry for you at dinner.'

'I think he was meaning to be kind,' Lucy replied.

'I'm sure he was,' said Miss Bartlett. 'I was just being careful for my cousin's sake.'

'Of course,' said the little old lady, and they murmured that one could not be too careful with a young girl.

Mr Beebe reappeared, looking extremely happy.

'Miss Bartlett,' he cried. 'It's all right about the rooms. I'm so glad. Mr Emerson was talking about it in the smoking room, and as I knew what had happened, I encouraged him to make the offer again. He has allowed me to come and ask you. He would be so pleased.'

'Oh, Charlotte!' cried Lucy to her cousin. 'We must have the rooms now. The old man is so nice and kind.'

Miss Bartlett was silent.

'I am afraid,' said Mr Beebe, after a pause, 'that I have done the wrong thing. I apologise.'

Very cross, he turned to go. At that moment Miss Bartlett replied, 'My own wishes are not important when compared to yours, Lucy. I am only here because of your kindness. Will you, Mr Beebe, please tell Mr Emerson that I accept his kind offer, and then take me to him so I can thank him personally?'

Mr Beebe bowed, and departed with her message.

He returned, saying rather nervously, 'Mr Emerson is busy, but here is his son instead.'

'My father,' the young man said, 'is in his bath, so you cannot thank him personally. But I will give him the message as soon as he comes out.'

Miss Bartlett was embarrassed by the mention of the bath. It was a victory for George, to the delight of Mr Beebe and the secret delight of Lucy. After George had left, they waited for half an hour for their new rooms to be prepared.

'I think we could go now,' Miss Bartlett said at last. 'No, Lucy, don't move. I will organise the move.'

'You do everything,' said Lucy.

'Naturally, dear. It is my duty.'

'But I would like to help you.'

'No, dear.'

Charlotte's energy! And her unselfishness! She had been like this all her life, but especially on this Italian tour. But although

Lucy felt this, or tried to feel this, there was a rebellious part of her which wondered whether Charlotte could not have behaved in a more attractive way. She entered her bedroom with no feeling of joy.

'I want to explain,' said Miss Bartlett, 'why I have taken the largest room. I know that it belonged to the young man, and I was sure that your mother would not like it.'

Lucy was puzzled. 'Mother wouldn't mind, I'm sure,' she said, but she had a feeling that something more important and unsuspected was involved.

Miss Bartlett sighed, and put her arms around Lucy as she wished her goodnight. It gave Lucy the sensation of a fog, and when she reached her own room, she opened the window and breathed the clean night air, thinking of the kind old man who had enabled her to see the lights dancing in the river, and the trees and hills in the distance, black against the rising moon.

Miss Bartlett, in her room, closed the windows and locked the door. Inspecting her room, she noticed a sheet of paper, pinned up on the wall. On it was written an enormous question mark. Nothing more.

'What does it mean?' she thought, and examined it carefully. She wanted to destroy it, but remembered that she did not have the right to do so, since it must be the property of young Mr Emerson. So she took it down and put it between two pieces of paper to keep it clean for him. Then she completed her inspection of the room, sighed heavily and went to bed.

Chapter 2   In Santa Croce without a Guidebook

It was pleasant to wake up in Florence, to open one's eyes upon a bright, bare room, and look at a ceiling painted with animals and musical instruments. It was pleasant, too, to throw open the windows, to lean out into sunshine with beautiful hills and trees and churches opposite, and, below, the river.

Over the river men were at work with spades on the sandy shore, and on the river there was a boat. An electric tram came rushing underneath the window. No one was inside it, except one tourist, but its platforms were overflowing with Italians, who preferred to stand. Children tried to hang on behind, and the ticket-collector tried to make them let go. Then soldiers appeared, good-looking, undersized men – each wearing a coat which had been made for a larger soldier. Behind them walked officers, looking fierce, and in front of them went little boys, jumping up and down in time with the band. The tram became stuck and moved on slowly. One of the little boys fell down, and some white cows came out of an entrance. In fact, if it had not been for the good advice of an old man selling souvenirs, the road might never have got clear.

Looking at such everyday scenes as this, many a valuable hour can disappear, and the traveller who has gone to Italy to study Giotto,★ or the history of the Church, may return home remembering nothing except the blue sky and the men and women who live under it. So it was a good thing that Miss Bartlett tapped on Lucy's door and came in. After commenting on Lucy having left the door unlocked, and leaning out of the window before she was fully dressed, Miss Bartlett encouraged her to hurry, or the best part of the day would be gone. By the time Lucy was ready, her cousin had finished her breakfast, and was listening to the clever lady whom they had met the previous night.

A familiar sort of conversation followed. Miss Bartlett was, after all, a little tired, and thought they had better spend the morning settling in – unless Lucy would like to go out? Lucy

★Giotto: a famous Italian painter and architect who lived in the thirteenth and fourteenth centuries

would rather like to go out, as it was her first day in Florence, but, of course, she could go alone. Miss Bartlett could not allow this. Of course she would accompany Lucy everywhere. Oh, certainly not; Lucy would stay with her cousin. Oh no! That was not possible! Oh yes!

At this moment, the clever lady interrupted. 'I do assure you that, being English, Miss Honeychurch will be perfectly safe. Italians understand.'

Miss Bartlett was not persuaded. She was determined to take Lucy herself.

The clever lady then said that she was going to spend a long morning in the church of Santa Croce, and if Lucy would come too she would be delighted. 'I will take you by a dear, dirty back way, Miss Honeychurch, and if you bring me luck, we shall have an adventure.'

Lucy said that this was most kind, and at once opened the guidebook to see where Santa Croce was. She hurried to finish her breakfast, and left the pension with her new friend feeling happy. She felt at last that she really was in Italy. The Signora and the events of the evening before had disappeared like a bad dream.

Miss Lavish – that was the clever lady's name – turned right outside the pension. How warm it was! Look, there was Ponte alle Grazie, a particularly interesting bridge, mentioned by the poet Dante. Then Miss Lavish ran through the entrance where Lucy had seen the cows earlier, stopped and cried, 'A smell! A true Florentine smell! Every city, let me teach you, has its own smell.'

'Is it a very nice smell?' said Lucy, who, like her mother, disliked dirt.

'One does not come to Italy for niceness,' Miss Lavish replied. 'One comes for life. *Buon giorno!*★ *Buon giorno!*' She bowed left and right.

★*Buon giorno!*: the Italian for 'Good morning!'

Miss Lavish proceeded through the streets of the city of Florence, as playful as a child. It was a treat for the girl to be with someone so clever and so cheerful.

'*Buon giorno!* Believe an old woman, Miss Lucy: you will never be sorry if you are polite to everyone you meet.'

They talked about Lucy's home in England, in Summer Street, and found they knew some of the same people. And just as Miss Lavish remembered the name of someone who had rented a house in Summer Street, she suddenly stopped and exclaimed, 'Oh dear! We are lost!'

Certainly they had seemed to take a long time to reach Santa Croce; the church tower could be seen from the pension window. But Miss Lavish had said so much about knowing Florence that Lucy had followed her without question.

Lucy suggested that they should ask someone the way.

'That is what a coward would say! We will simply wander.'

And they wandered through a series of grey-brown streets, which were not pretty, in the eastern part of the city. Lucy became discontented. The ladies bought a snack at a little shop, because it looked typically Italian. It gave them strength to walk on into another square, large and dusty, on the other side of which rose a very ugly black and white church. It was Santa Croce. The adventure was over. They saw old Mr Emerson and his son George ahead of them.

The two ladies were going to enter the church, when Miss Lavish stopped and cried, 'There goes someone I must speak to!' And in a moment she was running across the square.

Lucy waited for nearly ten minutes. Then she began to get tired. The dust blew in her eyes, and she remembered that a young girl should not wait in public places. She started to walk towards Miss Lavish. But at that moment Miss Lavish disappeared down a side street.

Tears filled Lucy's eyes. She did not have her guidebook. How could she find her way home? How could she find her way about in the church? Her first morning was spoiled, and she might never be in Florence again. She entered the church feeling depressed, not even able to remember who had built it.

Of course, it must be a wonderful building. But how big! And how very cold! The church contained wall paintings by Giotto. But which were they? She walked around, unwilling to be enthusiastic about things that she knew nothing about.

Then the charm of Italy worked on her, and, instead of gathering information, she began to be happy. She managed to understand the Italian notices – notices that forbade people from bringing dogs into the church, or told people not to spit. She watched the tourists. Then a little boy tripped over the edge of a piece of stone. Lucy rushed forward. She was too late. The boy fell over.

'Go out into the sunshine, little boy,' exclaimed the voice of Mr Emerson, who had run forward as well.

The child screamed at these words, and at the strange people. Each time that old Mr Emerson and Lucy tried to pick him up, he fell down again. His mother came to the rescue.

'What are you doing here?' asked Mr Emerson. 'Are you looking at the church?'

'No,' cried Lucy. 'I came with Miss Lavish, who was going to explain everything, and – it is too bad! – she just ran away, and after waiting a long time, I had to come in by myself.'

'Why shouldn't you?' said Mr Emerson.

'Yes, why shouldn't you come by yourself?' said his son, George, speaking to Lucy for the first time that day. 'You can join us.'

'Thank you very much, but I could not think of that.'

'My dear,' said the old man gently, 'I think you are repeating what you have heard older people say. Stop being so difficult, and tell me instead what part of the church you want to see. To take you to it will be a real pleasure.'

Now, this was not polite, and she ought to have been cross. But Lucy could not get cross. Mr Emerson was an old man. She looked at his son.

'I am not difficult, I hope. It is the Giottos that I want to see, if you will kindly tell me which they are.'

The son nodded and led the way to the paintings. There was a crowd of people and, in the middle, a lecturer talking about them. Mr Emerson disagreed with something the lecturer said, and insisted in a voice which was much too loud, 'This church wasn't built by faith. That simply means the workmen weren't paid properly. And I don't see any truth in the paintings. Look at that fat man in blue! He must weigh as much as I do.'

The lecturer paused. Lucy was sure she should not be with these two men, but she was under their spell. They were so serious and strange that she could not remember how to behave. Father and son continued talking to each other about the paintings.

'Excuse me,' said a cold voice. 'This space is too small for all of us. We will not stay in your way any longer.'

The lecturer was a clergyman, and he and his group walked away. Among them were the two little old ladies from the Pension Bertolini, Miss Teresa and Miss Catharine Alan.

'Stop!' cried Mr Emerson. 'There's plenty of room for us all. Stop!'

The group disappeared without a word.

'George,' said Mr Emerson, 'I do believe that clergyman is from Brixton. I must speak to him and remind him who I am. It's Mr Eager. Why did he go? Did we talk too loudly? I shall go and say we are sorry. Then perhaps he will come back.'

'He will not come back,' said George.

But Mr Emerson, unhappy, hurried away to apologise.

'My father insists on being kind,' George informed Lucy.

'I hope we all try to do that,' she said, smiling nervously.

Mr Emerson returned. 'We have spoiled the pleasure of many people. They won't come back.' They could hear Mr Eager talking about St★ Francis nearby. He continued to Lucy, 'Don't let us spoil your day. Have you looked at these saints?'

'Yes,' said Lucy. 'They are lovely.'

George did not want to look at anything else, and Lucy and the old man wandered around the church. Mr Emerson looked back at his son.

'My boy is unhappy.'

'Oh dear!' said Lucy.

'How can he be unhappy when he is strong and alive? What more can one give him? And think how I have brought him up, not having to believe in God. I thought he would grow up happy.'

Lucy thought he was very irreligious. She also felt that her mother would not like her talking to that kind of person, and Charlotte would object very strongly.

Suddenly Mr Emerson said, 'Now don't be stupid over this. I don't require you to fall in love with my boy, but I do think you could try to understand him. You are nearer his age, and if you allow yourself to relax, I am sure you are sensible. You can help me. He has known so few women, and you have the time. But relax. Your thinking is sometimes rather muddled. But by understanding George, you may learn to understand yourself. It will be good for both of you.'

To this extraordinary speech, Lucy found no answer.

'I only know what it is that's wrong with him; not why it is. It is the fact that things in this world around us don't make sense to him. Why should this make him unhappy?'

Suddenly Lucy laughed. 'I'm very sorry,' she cried. 'You'll think I am unsympathetic, but – but – ' Then, sounding like her

★St: the short form of the word 'Saint'

mother, she said, 'Oh, but your son needs employment. Has he no particular hobby? I myself have worries, but I can generally forget them at the piano. Collecting stamps helped my brother a lot.'

The old man looked sad, and he touched her gently with his hand as George came towards them.

George said, 'Miss Bartlett.'

'Oh goodness! Where? Where?' asked Lucy. 'I see. Those gossiping Miss Alans must have – '

'Poor girl!' exploded old Mr Emerson. 'Poor girl!'

She could not stay silent; secretly she agreed with him. 'Poor girl? I don't understand. I think I am a very fortunate girl, I assure you. I'm very happy and having a lovely time. Please don't waste time worrying about *me*. Thank you both so much for all your kindness. Ah yes! There is my cousin. Santa Croce is a wonderful church.'

She rejoined Charlotte.

Chapter 3   Lucy Witnesses a Tragedy

A very wet afternoon at the Bertolini permitted Lucy to do the thing she really liked, and after lunch she opened the little piano and played some Beethoven. A few people listened and praised her playing, but, finding that she made no reply, went to their rooms to write their diaries or to sleep. She took no notice of Mr Emerson looking for his son, nor of Miss Bartlett looking for Miss Lavish, nor of Miss Lavish looking for her cigarette case. Like every true performer, she was excited just by the feel of the notes; they were like fingers touching her own. It was the touch as well as the sound that satisfied her.

Mr Beebe, sitting unnoticed by the window, remembered the occasion at an entertainment in Tunbridge Wells when he had first met Lucy and discovered her piano-playing. The local vicar had told him about her.

'She's the cousin of Miss Bartlett, who lives in this parish. They are both full of praise for your sermon.'

'My sermon?' cried Mr Beebe. 'Why did she listen to that?'

When he was introduced, he understood why; Miss Honeychurch was only a young lady with a quantity of dark hair and a very pretty, pale, undeveloped face. She loved going to concerts, she loved staying with her cousin, she loved iced coffee and cakes. He did not doubt that she loved his sermon also. But before he left Tunbridge Wells, he made a remark to the vicar which he now made to Lucy herself when she closed the little piano and moved dreamily towards him.

'If Miss Honeychurch ever starts to live life as she plays the piano, it will be very exciting – both for us and for her.'

'Music – ' said Lucy, as if attempting a generality. She could not finish, and looked out upon Italy in the wet. The street and the river were dirty yellow, the hills a dirty purple. Somewhere in the hills were Miss Lavish and Miss Bartlett.

'What about music?' said Mr Beebe.

'Poor Charlotte will be very wet,' was Lucy's reply.

The expedition was typical of Miss Bartlett, who would return cold, tired and hungry, with a ruined skirt and an annoying cough. On another day, when the whole world was singing, she would refuse to move from the sitting room, saying that she was too old for a young girl's companion.

'Miss Lavish hopes to find the true Italy in the wet, I believe.'

'Is it true,' said Lucy, sounding very impressed, 'that Miss Lavish is writing a book?'

'A novel,' replied Mr Beebe.

'I do wish Miss Lavish would tell me about it herself. We started such friends. But I don't think she ought to have run away that morning in Santa Croce. Charlotte was most annoyed at finding me almost alone.'

'The two ladies, however, are friends again.'

Mr Beebe was interested in the sudden friendship between women so apparently dissimilar as Miss Bartlett and Miss Lavish. They were always in each other's company, with Lucy an excluded third. He believed he understood Miss Lavish, but Miss Bartlett might reveal unknown depths of strangeness. Was Italy affecting the role he had given her in Tunbridge Wells – the cautious chaperone? All his life he had loved to study unmarried ladies, and his profession had provided him with many opportunities. Girls like Lucy were charming to look at, but Mr Beebe was, for deep reasons, rather cold in his attitude towards the opposite sex, and preferred to remain interested rather than be involved.

Miss Catharine Alan entered. She sat down, self-conscious as she always was when she entered a room which contained a man.

'I could hear your beautiful playing, Miss Honeychurch, though I was in my room with the door shut.' She bent down and picked up a cigarette case. On it were the initials E.L.

'That belongs to Miss Lavish,' said the clergyman. 'She is a good person, but I wish she'd smoke a pipe.'

'Oh, Mr Beebe,' said Miss Alan. 'She started smoking when she was desperate, after her life's work was destroyed. Surely that makes it easier to excuse.'

'What was that?' asked Lucy.

Mr Beebe sat back, and Miss Alan began. 'It was a novel, and, I have been told, not a very nice novel. Anyway, she was writing in a cave near her seaside hotel and went for some ink. Meanwhile, the wall of the cave fell down, and her writing was swept away. It's a great secret, but I am glad to say that she is writing another novel, about modern Italy. She cannot start until she has had an idea, so she has come here. I cannot help thinking that there is something to admire in everyone, even if you do not approve of them. But she did behave most strangely when the Emersons arrived, taking part in unsuitable conversations, and joining them in the smoking room after dinner.'

Lucy asked, 'Mr Beebe – old Mr Emerson, is he nice or not? It is so difficult. Miss Alan, what do you think?'

The little old lady shook her head, and sighed disapprovingly. Mr Beebe, whom the conversation amused, wanted to see how she would react to his next remark. 'I consider that you should think him nice, Miss Alan, after that business with the violets.'

'Violets? Oh dear! Who told you about the violets? How people talk. No, I cannot forget how they behaved at Mr Eager's lecture at Santa Croce. No, I have quite changed. I do *not* like the Emersons. They are *not* nice.'

Mr Beebe smiled. He had made a gentle effort to introduce the Emersons into Bertolini society, and had failed. He was almost the only person who remained friendly to them.

Lucy, looking out at the weather, finally said that she thought the Emersons were nice, although she did not see them now. Even their seats at dinner had been moved.

Mr Beebe wondered whether to plan a pleasant day for the Emersons before they left – an expedition, perhaps, with Lucy well chaperoned to be nice to them. It was one of Mr Beebe's chief pleasures to provide people with happy memories.

Evening approached while they chatted. The air became brighter; the colours on the trees and hills were clear again.

'I think I shall go out,' said Lucy. 'I want to go round the town in the circular tram.'

Both her companions looked disapproving, so Lucy said that she would only go for a little walk, and stay on the streets that were full of tourists.

'She oughtn't really to go at all,' said Mr Beebe, as they watched her from the window, 'and she knows it. I blame the whole thing on too much Beethoven.'

◆

Mr Beebe was right. Lucy always knew her desires clearly after music. Conversation was boring; she wanted something big, and she believed that it would have come to her on the windy platform of an electric tram.

This she could not attempt. It was unladylike. Why? Why were most big things unladylike? Charlotte had once explained to her why. Ladies were not inferior to men; they were different. Their role was to help others achieve things, rather than to achieve themselves. Indirectly, in a tactful manner, a lady could do much. But if she rushed into things herself, she would be criticised, despised and finally ignored. Poems had been written to illustrate this point.

Lucy was not a rebel, but this afternoon she was particularly restless. She would really like to do something of which those who wished her well disapproved. As she was not able to go on the electric tram, she went to a shop and bought a photograph of Botticelli's painting, *Birth of Venus*. The figure of Venus was a pity and spoiled the painting, and Miss Bartlett had persuaded her not to buy it. (A 'pity' in art, of course, meant someone painted nude.) She bought more photographs, approving of everyone with a well known name.

But though she spent some of her Italian money, she was still aware of feeling discontented. It was new to her to be aware of this feeling. 'Nothing ever happens to me,' she reflected, as she entered the Piazza★ Signoria and looked at the marvellous things in it. The great square was in shadow. The tower of the palace rose out of the darkness; its brightness amazed her.

Then something did happen.

Two Italians had been arguing about money. They started to fight, and one was hit lightly on the chest. He bent towards Lucy with a look of interest, as if he had an important message for her. He opened his lips to deliver it, and a stream of red came out between them and ran down his unshaven chin.

★Piazza: the Italian word for a square

That was all. A crowd rose out of the dusk. It hid this extraordinary man from her, and carried him away to the fountain. Mr George Emerson appeared a few steps away. How very odd! Even as she saw him, he started to fade; the palace itself started to fade, moved above her, fell onto her softly, slowly, noiselessly, and the sky fell with it.

'Oh, what have I done?' she murmured, and opened her eyes.

She had complained of dullness, and suddenly one man was stabbed and another held her in his arms.

They were sitting on some steps. He must have carried her. He rose when she spoke, and began to dust his knees.

'Oh, what have I done?'

'You fainted.'

'I – I am very sorry.'

'How are you now?'

'Perfectly well.' And she began to nod and smile.

'Then let us go home. There's no point in staying.'

He held out his hand to pull her up. She pretended not to see it. The cries from the fountain rang out. The whole world seemed pale and without its original meaning.

'How very kind you have been. I might have hurt myself when I fell. But now I am well, I can go alone, thank you.'

His hand was still extended.

'Oh, my photographs!' she exclaimed suddenly. 'I must have dropped them out there in the square. She looked at him cautiously. 'Would you fetch them?'

As soon as he had turned around, Lucy got up and crept away.

'Miss Honeychurch!' She stopped with her hand on her heart. 'You sit still. You aren't fit to go home alone.'

'But I would rather – '

'Then I won't fetch your photographs.'

'I would rather be alone.'

He said forcefully, 'The man is probably dead. Sit down till you are rested.'

She was confused, and obeyed him. Again she thought, 'Oh, what have I done?' She felt that she, as well as the dying man, had crossed some spiritual boundary.

He returned, and she talked of the murder. Oddly, it was an easy topic. She became almost talkative over the incident that had made her faint five minutes before. Being strong physically, she soon overcame the horror of blood. She rose without his assistance, and though wings seemed to beat inside her, she walked firmly enough towards the river. A cab-driver signalled to them; they refused him.

'And the murderer tried to kiss him, you say – how very odd Italians are! – and gave himself up to the police! Mr Beebe was saying that Italians know everything . . . What was that?'

He had thrown something into the river.

'Things I didn't want,' he said crossly.

'Mr Emerson! Where are the photographs?'

He was silent.

'I believe it was my photographs that you threw away.'

'I didn't know what to do with them,' he cried, and his voice was that of an anxious boy. Her heart warmed towards him for the first time. 'They were covered with blood. Now, I'm glad I've told you; and all the time we were making conversation, I was wondering what to do with them.' He pointed down at the river. 'They've gone. I did mind about them, and one is so foolish, it seemed better that they should go out to the sea. I don't know – I may just mean that they frightened me.' Then the boy turned into a man. 'Something tremendous has happened; I must face it without getting muddled.'

'Mr Emerson, I want to ask you something before we go in.'

They were close to their pension. She stopped and leant her elbows on the stone wall above the river. He did the same. It is sometimes magical when two people take the same position. It suggests a friendship that will last for ever. She moved her elbows before saying, 'I was never so ashamed of myself in my life. I cannot think what happened to me.'

'I nearly fainted myself,' he said, but she felt that her attitude disgusted him.

'Well, I owe you a thousand apologies. And you know how silly people gossip – ladies especially, I am afraid. Would you not mention it to anyone, my foolish behaviour?'

'Your behaviour? Oh yes, all right – all right.'

The river was flowing below them, almost black in the advancing night. He had thrown her photographs into it, and then he had told her the reason. He would do no harm with unnecessary gossip; he could be trusted, he was intelligent, and even kind. But he lacked an understanding of correct behaviour; his thoughts, like his behaviour, would not be changed by worrying about what was right. She had been in his arms, and he remembered it, just as he remembered the blood on the photographs. It was not exactly that a man had died; something had happened to the living.

'Well, thank you so much,' she repeated. 'How quickly these accidents happen, and then one returns to the old life.'

His answer puzzled her. 'I don't. I shall probably want to live.'

'But why, Mr Emerson? What do you mean?'

'I mean I shall want to live.'

Leaning her elbows on the wall, she looked at the river, whose roar suggested some unexpected music to her ears.

Chapter 4   Possibilities of a Pleasant Outing

It was always said in the family that 'you never knew how Charlotte Bartlett would react'. She was perfectly pleasant and sensible about Lucy's adventure, found the shortened version of it quite adequate, and was suitably appreciative of Mr George Emerson's help.

For good or evil, Lucy was left to face her problem alone. None of her friends had seen her, either in the square or later, by the river. Mr Beebe, noticing her bright eyes at dinner time, had again thought to himself, 'too much Beethoven'. But he only supposed that she was ready for an adventure, not that she had already had one. This isolation depressed Lucy; she was accustomed to having her thoughts confirmed by others, or at least challenged. It was awful not to know whether what she was thinking was right or wrong.

At breakfast next morning, she took decisive action. There were two plans between which she had to choose. Mr Beebe was walking up to the Torre del Gallo* with the Emersons and some American ladies. Would Miss Bartlett and Miss Honeychurch join the party? Charlotte refused the invitation for herself; she had been there in the rain the previous afternoon. But she thought it an admirable idea for Lucy, who hated shopping, changing money, fetching letters and other boring duties – all of which Miss Bartlett must do this morning, and could easily do alone.

'No, Charlotte!' cried the girl, with real warmth. 'It's very kind of Mr Beebe, but I would rather come with you.'

'Very well, dear,' said Miss Bartlett, looking a little pleased.

Lucy felt ashamed. How badly she behaved to Charlotte, now as always! But she would alter. All morning she would be really nice to her.

She slipped her arm into her cousin's, and they set off along the river. Miss Bartlett insisted on leaning over the wall to look at it. She then made her usual remark, which was, 'How I wish Freddy and your mother could see this too!'

Lucy was a little annoyed that Charlotte had stopped exactly where she did.

*Torre del Gallo: a fourteenth-century tower

23

'Look, Lucy! Oh, you are watching for the Torre del Gallo party. I feared that you would regret your choice.'

Although the choice had been serious, Lucy did not regret it. Yesterday had been a muddle – strange and odd, the kind of thing that one could not write down easily on paper – but she had a feeling that Charlotte and her shopping were preferable to George Emerson and the top of the Torre del Gallo. Since she could not understand what had happened, she must be careful not to get in a muddle again.

But although she had avoided the main actor from yesterday, the scenery unfortunately remained. Charlotte, for some unknown reason, led her from the river to the Piazza Signoria. Lucy could not have believed that stones, a fountain, a palace tower, would be so significant to her. For a moment she understood the nature of ghosts.

The exact site of the murder was occupied, not by a ghost, but by Miss Lavish, who had the morning newspaper in her hand. She waved at them. The awful tragedy of the previous day had given her an idea, which she thought she could put into a book.

'Oh, let me congratulate you!' said Miss Bartlett. 'You felt so desperate yesterday! What a fortunate thing!'

'Ah! Miss Honeychurch, you have come back! I am in luck. Now, you must tell me absolutely everything that you saw.'

Lucy looked down at the ground.

'But perhaps you would rather not?'

'I'm sorry – if you could manage without it, I think I would rather not.'

The older ladies looked at each other. They did not disapprove. It is suitable that a girl should feel deeply.

'It is I who am sorry,' said Miss Lavish. 'We writers behave badly. There is no secret of the human heart that we do not wish to investigate.'

She marched cheerfully to the fountain and back, and did a few calculations. Then she said that she had been in the square since eight o'clock, collecting material for her book. A good deal of it was unsuitable, but of course one always had to adapt. The two men had quarrelled over a debt. She would change the debt to a young lady, which would make it more tragic, and also provide her with an excellent plot.

'What is the heroine's name?' asked Miss Bartlett.

'Leonora,' said Miss Lavish; her own name was Eleanor.

'I do hope she's nice. And what is the plot?'

Love, murder, kidnapping, revenge, was the plot. She explained it while the fountain splashed in the morning sun.

'I hope you will forgive me for being so boring,' Miss Lavish said. 'It is so tempting to talk to really sympathetic people. Of course, I have only described the main idea. There will be a great deal of detail about Florence, and the neighbourhood, and I shall also introduce some humorous characters. And let me give you all a warning; I do not intend to be kind to the British tourist.'

'Oh, you wicked woman!' cried Miss Bartlett. 'I am sure you are thinking of the Emersons.'

'I confess that in Italy, I do not feel very sympathetic to my own countrymen. It is the Italians who attract me, and whose lives I am going to paint as well as I can. I repeat and I insist, and I have always believed most strongly, that yesterday's tragedy is not less tragic because it happened in humble life.'

There was silence. Then the cousins wished her success, and walked slowly away across the square.

'She is my idea of a really clever woman,' said Miss Bartlett.

Lucy agreed. At present, her main aim was not to be put into Miss Lavish's book. She believed that Miss Lavish was thinking about her as the heroine.

'We had a long talk yesterday. She told me that she has a high opinion of the future role of women – Mr Eager! How nice! What a pleasant surprise!'

'Ah, not for me,' said the clergyman. 'I have been watching you and Miss Honeychurch for some time.'

'We were chatting to Miss Lavish.'

'So I saw. I am going to make a suggestion. Would you and Miss Honeychurch like to join me in a drive one day this week – a drive in the hills? We could go up by Fiesole and back by Settignano. There is a place on that road where we could stop and walk on the hillside. The view of Florence is most beautiful – much better than the view from Fiesole.'

Miss Bartlett knew that Mr Eager was no ordinary vicar. He was a member of the English community who had made Florence their home. He knew the people who never walked around with guidebooks, who had learned to rest after lunch, who went on drives the ordinary tourists did not know about, and were allowed into galleries that were normally closed. They lived in flats, or villas in the hills; they read, wrote, studied and exchanged ideas, and so had a knowledge of Florence which was denied to the normal traveller.

Therefore an invitation from the vicar was something to be proud of. Between the two groups of English people, the residents and the tourists, he was often the only link. He liked to select one or two of the tourists who he thought deserved it, and take them to spend a few hours in the places that the residents knew. Nothing had been mentioned yet about tea at a villa. But if it happened – how Lucy would enjoy it!

A few days ago, Lucy would have felt the same. But the joys of life were changing. A drive in the hills with Mr Eager and Miss Bartlett – even if it ended in tea with the residents – was no longer the most wonderful event. She echoed Charlotte's delight rather faintly. It was not until she heard that Mr Beebe was coming that her thanks became more sincere.

'This square – so I am told – witnessed yesterday a terrible tragedy,' continued Mr Eager.

'It did,' said Miss Bartlett. 'Miss Honeychurch was passing through as it happened. She cannot really speak about it.' She glanced at Lucy proudly.

'So you were here alone, Miss Honeychurch?' His voice indicated that he would be interested in some details.

'Almost alone.'

'One of the other people from the pension kindly brought her home,' said Miss Bartlett, cleverly hiding the sex of the person.

'For her also it must have been a terrible experience. I hope that neither of you were at all – that you were not too close.'

One of the many things that Lucy was noticing today was the way in which respectable people were interested in blood. George Emerson had kept the subject strangely pure.

'He died by the fountain, I believe,' was her reply.

'And you and your friend – '

'We were at the side of the square.'

A man started trying to sell them photographs. 'Ignore him,' said Mr Eager, and they all walked away from the square.

Shopping was the topic that now followed. Guided by Mr Eager, they selected many ugly presents and souvenirs – all of which would have cost less in London.

This successful morning did not leave a good impression on Lucy. She had been a little frightened, both by Miss Lavish and by Mr Eager; she did not know why. And as they frightened her she had, strangely enough, stopped respecting them. She doubted that Miss Lavish was a great writer. She doubted that Mr Eager was as spiritual and cultured as she had been told. And Charlotte – Charlotte was exactly the same. It might be possible to be nice to her; it was impossible to love her.

Miss Bartlett and Mr Eager were talking about the Emersons.

'Old Mr Emerson is the son of a labourer. He was a mechanic of some sort when he was young. Then he was a journalist for a Socialist newspaper,' said Mr Eager.

'How wonderfully people can move up in society these days,' sighed Miss Bartlett, picking up a model tower.

'Old Mr Emerson's marriage was an advantage to him.' Mr Eager made this remark sound very important.

'Oh, so he has a wife,' said Charlotte.

'Dead, Miss Bartlett, dead. I wonder – yes, I wonder – how he dares to look at me and say that we know each other. He was in my London parish a long time ago. The other day in Santa Croce, I refused to speak to him. He should be careful that I do no more.'

'What?' cried Lucy.

Mr Eager tried to change the subject, but his audience were more interested than he had intended. Miss Bartlett was full of natural curiosity. Lucy, though she never wanted to see the Emersons again, did not want to dismiss them so quickly.

'Perhaps,' said Miss Bartlett, 'it is something that we had better not hear.'

'To speak plainly,' said Mr Eager, 'it is. I will say no more.'

For the first time, Lucy's rebellious thoughts were turned into words – for the first time in her life.

'You have said very little.'

'It was my intention to say little,' was his cold reply. Lucy turned towards him. It was terrible that she did not believe him. 'Murder, if you want to know,' he cried angrily. 'That man murdered his wife! You will find it difficult to defend him. That man murdered his wife in the sight of God.'

Miss Bartlett quickly bought the model tower, and led the way into the street.

'I must be going,' said Mr Eager, covering his eyes from the sun and looking at his watch.

Miss Bartlett thanked him for his kindness, and spoke enthusiastically about the drive.

'Drive? Oh, are we going on the drive?'

Lucy remembered her manners and, after a little effort, Mr Eager's good humour returned.

When he had left, Miss Bartlett and Lucy went to the post office. There were letters from home for Lucy.

'And the news?' asked Miss Bartlett.

'Mrs Vyse and her son have gone to Rome.' Lucy gave the news that she found least interesting. 'Do you know the Vyses? They're nice people. So clever – my idea of what's really clever. Don't you long to be in Rome?'

'I die for it!'

'Charlotte!' cried the girl suddenly. 'Here's an idea. Shall we go to Rome tomorrow – straight to the Vyses' hotel? I know what I want. I'm bored of Florence.'

Miss Bartlett replied, 'Oh, you funny person! What would happen about your drive in the hills?'

They both laughed at the impractical suggestion.

Chapter 5   The English Guests Drive Out in Carriages

It was a young Italian who drove them in carriages to Fiesole that day, an irresponsible youth who drove the horses in a wild manner up the stony hill. On the way, he asked if he could collect a girl to accompany him, saying that she was his sister. Mr Eager objected, but the ladies supported him and the girl was allowed to join him. He drove with one arm round her waist. Mr Eager, who sat with his back to the horses, saw nothing and continued talking to Lucy. The other two people in that carriage were old Mr Emerson and Miss Lavish.

An awful thing had happened. Mr Beebe, without consulting Mr Eager, had doubled the size of the party. And though Miss Bartlett and Miss Lavish had planned how people would sit, when the carriages arrived they got in a muddle. Miss Lavish and Mr Emerson got in with Lucy. Miss Bartlett, George Emerson and Mr Beebe followed on behind in a second carriage.

It was difficult for Mr Eager to have his expedition altered. It would now be impossible to have tea at a villa. Lucy and Miss Bartlett had a certain style, and Mr Beebe, though unreliable, was acceptable. But he could not introduce a lady writer like Miss Lavish, or a journalist who had murdered his wife in the sight of God, to any of the English residents.

Lucy, elegantly dressed in white, sat nervously in the group. Without this expedition, she could have avoided George Emerson successfully. He had shown that he wished to continue their friendship. She had refused, not because she disliked him, but because she did not know what had happened, and suspected he did know. This frightened her.

It frightened her because the real event – whatever it was – had taken place, not in the square, but by the river. To behave wildly at the sight of death can be forgiven. But to discuss it afterwards, to share and reflect on the experience together, that is wrong. Each time that she avoided George, it became more important that she should avoid him again.

Meanwhile, Mr Eager talked to her; their little argument was over. 'So, Miss Honeychurch, you travel as a student of art?'

'Oh, no – no! I am here as a tourist.'

'Are you really?' said Mr Eager. 'If you will not think me rude, we residents sometimes pity you poor tourists, living together in pensions or hotels, quite unconscious of anything that is outside your guidebook. The English community in Florence, Miss Honeychurch, is quite large, though not everyone is from the same background. But most of them are students. Lady Helen Laverstock is at present studying Fra Angelico* – we are passing her villa on the left.'

*Fra Angelico: a famous fifteenth-century Italian painter

During this speech, the two figures at the front of the carriage were behaving very badly. Lucy felt a stab of envy. They were probably the only people enjoying the expedition.

The other carriage was left behind. As the horses went faster, the large, sleeping figure of Mr Emerson was thrown against Mr Eager. The boy driving, who had been trying to kiss the girl beside him, had just succeeded.

A little scene followed. The horses were stopped, the lovers ordered to separate, the boy would not receive a tip.

'She is my sister,' said the boy, looking at them with sad eyes. Mr Eager told him that he was not telling the truth.

The other carriage had stopped behind them, and sensible Mr Beebe called out that after this warning he was sure that the couple would behave themselves properly.

'Leave them alone,' begged Mr Emerson, who was not frightened by Mr Eager. 'It would be wrong to separate them.'

The voice of Miss Bartlett could be heard saying that a crowd had gathered.

Mr Eager was determined to be heard. He spoke to the driver again; the girl got down from the carriage.

'Victory at last!' said Mr Eager, clapping his hands.

'It is not victory,' said Mr Emerson. 'It is defeat. You have separated two people who were happy.'

Mr Eager shut his eyes. He had to sit next to Mr Emerson, but he would not speak to him.

The old man commanded Lucy to agree with him and shouted for support to his son. 'We have tried to buy what cannot be bought with money. He agreed to drive us, and he is. We have no rights over his soul.'

No one encouraged him to talk. After a while, Mr Eager gave a signal for the carriages to stop, and organised the party for their walk on the hill. Everyone wandered around, their anxiety to keep together equalled by their desire to go in different directions. Finally, they split into groups. Lucy stayed with Miss Bartlett and Miss Lavish.

The two older ladies, in a loud whisper, began to discuss the drive. Miss Bartlett had asked Mr George Emerson what his profession was and he had answered 'the railway'. She had no idea that it would be such an awful answer, or she would not have asked him.

'The railway!' said Miss Lavish. 'Oh, but I shall die! Of course it was the railway!' She could not control her laughter. 'He looks just like a porter.'

'Eleanor, be quiet. They'll hear – the Emersons – '

'I'm sure it's all right,' said Lucy. 'The Emersons won't hear, and they wouldn't mind if they did.'

Miss Lavish did not seem pleased at this. 'Miss Honeychurch listening!' she said rather crossly. 'Naughty girl! Go away!'

'Oh, Lucy, you ought to be with Mr Eager, I'm sure.'

The girl refused to go.

'Then sit down,' said Miss Lavish. Smiling, she produced two scarves. She sat on one; who should sit on the other?

'Lucy,' said Miss Bartlett. 'I'll sit on the ground.' She sat down where the ground looked particularly damp and cleared her throat. 'Don't be alarmed. This is the tiniest cough, and I have had it for three days. It's nothing to do with sitting here.'

There was only one way of dealing with the situation. Lucy departed in search of Mr Beebe and Mr Eager.

She asked one of the drivers. '*Dove?*'*

His face lit up. He wanted to help her. But he needed to know more. Lucy could not remember the Italian for 'clergymen'. '*Dove buoni uomini?*' she said at last. In less than a quarter of a minute the driver was ready to accompany her. Italians are born knowing

---

*_Dove? Dove buoni uomini? Eccolo!_: the Italian for 'Where?' 'Where good men?' 'There!'

the way. He only stopped once, to pick her some great blue violets. She thanked him with real pleasure. In the company of this ordinary man the world was beautiful. For the first time she felt the influence of spring.

The rough grass became thicker and thicker. They could begin to see the view, but the bushes broke it into pieces.

There was a voice in the wood, in the distance behind them. The voice of Mr Eager? They could see the view at last.

'*Eccolo!*' the driver cried.

At the same moment, the ground gave way, and with a cry Lucy fell out of the wood. Light and beauty surrounded her. She had fallen onto a piece of open grass, which was covered with violets from end to end. From her feet the ground sloped sharply into the view. Standing at the edge was a man. But it was not whom she had expected, and he was alone.

George had turned at the sound of her arrival. For a moment he looked at her, as one who had fallen out of heaven. He saw joy in her face, he saw the flowers beat against her dress in blue waves. The bushes above them closed. He stepped quickly forward and kissed her.

Before she could speak, almost before she could feel, a voice called, 'Lucy! Lucy! Lucy!' The silence had been broken by Miss Bartlett, who stood against the view.

◆

Some complicated game had been played on the hillside all afternoon. What it was, and whose side the players had been on, Lucy was slow to discover. Mr Eager had met them with a questioning eye. Mr Beebe was told to collect the different groups for the journey home. He had lost everyone. Miss Lavish had lost Miss Bartlett, Lucy had lost Mr Eager, Mr Emerson had lost George. Miss Bartlett had lost a scarf.

The driver climbed onto the carriage. Bad weather was rapidly approaching. 'Let us go immediately,' he told them.

'The *signorino*★ wants to walk.'

Lucy sat beside Miss Bartlett as they journeyed down towards the fading sun. Mr Eager sat opposite, trying to catch her eye; he was a little suspicious.

Rain and darkness arrived together. There was a flash of lightning, and Miss Lavish, who was nervous, screamed from the carriage in front. At the next flash, Lucy screamed also.

Under the blanket, Lucy felt her cousin squeeze her hand kindly. Miss Bartlett achieved a great deal with this sympathetic gesture.

The carriages stopped, halfway to Florence.

'Mr Eager,' called Mr Beebe. 'We want your assistance. Will you help us?'

'George!' cried Mr Emerson. 'Ask your driver which way George went. The boy may lose his way. He may be killed.'

There was an explosion up the road. The storm had struck an overhead wire, and one of the great supports had fallen. If they had not stopped, perhaps they might have been hurt. They descended from the carriages, they embraced each other. For a moment they realised great possibilities of goodness.

Lucy said with emotion, 'Charlotte, dear Charlotte, kiss me. I have been silly – worse than you know. Once, by the river – oh, but he isn't killed – he wouldn't be killed, would he?'

'I hope not. One would always pray for that not to happen.'

'He is really – I think he was taken by surprise, just as I was before. But this time, I can't be blamed; I do want you to believe that. I simply slipped into those violets. No, I want to be really truthful. I can be blamed a little. I had silly thoughts.' Lucy's body was shaken with deep sighs. 'I want to be truthful,' she whispered. 'It's so hard to be absolutely truthful.'

★*Signorino*: an Italian word for a young man

'Don't be troubled, dearest. Wait till you are calmer. We will talk about it before bedtime in my room.'

So they re-entered the city holding hands. It was a shock to the girl to find how far emotion had faded in others. The storm had stopped and Mr Emerson was less worried about his son.

She was sure only of Charlotte – Charlotte, whose appearance hid so much understanding and love.

The luxury of a future confession kept Lucy almost happy throughout the long evening. She thought not so much about what had happened as of how she should describe it. All her sensations should be carefully told to her cousin. And together, they would understand it all.

'At last,' Lucy thought, 'I shall understand myself. I shan't again be troubled by things that come out of nothing, when I don't know what they mean.'

It was not until late that evening that Miss Bartlett suggested it was time for bed. Inviting Lucy into her room, Miss Bartlett shut the door, and said, 'So, what can we do?'

Lucy was unprepared for the question. It had not occurred to her that she would have to do anything.

'How are you going to stop Mr George Emerson talking?'

'I have a feeling that talk is a thing he will never do.' An idea rushed across Lucy's brain. 'I propose to speak to him.'

Miss Bartlett uttered a cry of genuine alarm. 'But I am frightened of him on your behalf, dear. You are so young and inexperienced, you have lived among such nice people, that you cannot realise what men can be. This afternoon, for example, if I had not arrived, what would have happened?'

'I have no idea,' said Lucy, seriously.

'When he insulted you, how would you have replied?'

'I would have – ' She stopped, went up to the window and looked into the darkness. She could not think what she would have done.

Miss Bartlett said, 'It will be a rush to catch the morning train to Rome, but we must try.'

The girl received the announcement calmly. 'What time does the train to Rome go?' she asked.

'At eight. Dearest Lucy,' said Miss Bartlett, 'how will you ever forgive me? I feel that our tour together is not the success I had hoped. I am too uninteresting and old-fashioned. I have been a failure. I have failed to make you happy and failed in my duty to your mother. She has been so generous to me; I shall never face her again after this disaster.'

Lucy, from a cowardly wish to improve the situation, said, 'Why need Mother hear about it? But in case she should blame you in any way, I promise I will never speak of it either to her or to anyone.'

Her promise brought the interview to an end. Miss Bartlett wished her goodnight, and sent her to her own room.

Some time later, she heard Miss Bartlett open her own door, and say, 'I wish to speak with you in the sitting room, Mr Emerson, please.'

Soon their footsteps returned, and Miss Bartlett said, 'Good night, Mr Emerson.'

His heavy, tired breathing was the only reply; the chaperone had done her work.

Lucy cried aloud, 'It isn't true. It can't all be true. I don't want to be muddled. I want to grow older quickly.'

Miss Bartlett tapped on the wall. 'Go to bed at once, dear. You need all the rest you can get.'

In the morning they left for Rome.

PART TWO The English in England

Chapter 6 Lucy's Engagement

Two pleasant people sat in the sitting room at Windy Corner. Lucy's brother, Freddy – a boy of nineteen – was studying a medical textbook. From time to time he sighed. The day was hot, the print in his book was small, and his mother, who was writing a letter, continually read out to him what she had written.

'I think something is going to happen,' said Mrs Honeychurch, walking to the window and looking out.

'It's time it did,' Freddy replied.

'I am glad that Cecil is asking her once more.'

'It's his third time, isn't it?'

'Freddy, I think the way you talk is unkind.'

'I didn't mean to be unkind.' Then he added, 'But I do think Lucy should have settled things in Italy. I don't know how girls manage things, but she can't have said 'no' properly before, or she wouldn't have to say it again now. I can't explain – I feel uncomfortable about the whole thing.'

He returned to his work.

'Just listen to what I have written to Mrs Vyse,' said his mother. 'I have said, "Dear Mrs Vyse. Cecil has just asked my permission about it and I would be delighted, if Lucy wishes it. But – "' She stopped reading. 'I was rather amused that Cecil asked my permission. He has always wanted to seem unconventional. In fact, he cannot arrange this without me.'

'Nor me.'

'You?'

Freddy nodded. 'He asked me for my permission also.'

Mrs Honeychurch exclaimed, 'How very odd! What do you know about Lucy or girls or anything? What did you say?'

'I said to Cecil, "It's your decision what you do. It's not my business." The bother is this . . .' began Freddy.

Then he started working again, too shy to say what the bother was. Mrs Honeychurch went back to the window.

'Freddy, you must come. They are still there!'

'I don't think you ought to look at them like that.'

'Can't I look out of my own window?'

But she returned to the writing table, observing, as she passed her son, 'Still on page 322?'

Freddy sighed, and turned over two pages. 'The bother is this,' he said. 'I have said the wrong thing to Cecil. He was not content with the "permission" I gave. He wanted to know if I was full of joy. He almost asked me whether I thought it was a splendid thing for Lucy and for Windy Corner generally if he married her. And he insisted on an answer.'

'I hope you gave a careful answer, dear.'

'I answered "no". I can't help it – I had to say it. I had to say no. He ought never to have asked me.'

'Ridiculous child!' cried his mother. 'You think you're so holy and truthful, but really it's terrible pride. Do you suppose that a man like Cecil would take the slightest notice of anything you say. How dare you say no?'

'Oh, do keep quiet, Mother! I had to say no when I couldn't say yes. I tried to laugh as if I didn't mean what I said, and, as Cecil laughed too, and went away, it may be all right. Oh, do keep quiet, though, and let me do some work.'

'No,' said Mrs Honeychurch. 'I shall not keep quiet. You know all that happened between Cecil and Lucy in Rome; you know why he is down here, but you insult him, and try to get him to leave my house.'

'It's not like that. I only said I didn't like him. I don't hate him. What worries me is that he'll tell Lucy.'

'Well, *I* like him,' said Mrs Honeychurch. 'I know his mother;

he's good, he's clever, he's rich, he knows the right sort of people. And he has beautiful manners.'

'I liked him till now. I suppose it's because he has spoiled Lucy's first week at home; and it's also something that Mr Beebe said, not knowing.'

'Mr Beebe?' said his mother.

'You know Mr Beebe's funny way, when you never quite know what he means. He said, "Mr Vyse is an ideal bachelor." I asked him what he meant. He said, "Oh, he's like me – better on his own." I couldn't make him say any more, but it made me think. Since Cecil has come after Lucy, he hasn't been so pleasant – I can't explain.'

'You never can, dear. But I can. You are jealous of Cecil because he may stop Lucy knitting you silk ties.'

Freddy tried to accept her explanation. Although he felt there was something he did not trust about Cecil, he could not think of a sensible reason why he disliked him. He must be jealous.

'Is this all right?' called his mother. ' "Dear Mrs Vyse, Cecil has just asked my permission about it, and I would be delighted if Lucy wishes it, and I have told Lucy so. But Lucy seems very uncertain, and in these days young people must decide for themselves. I know that Lucy likes your son, because she tells me everything. But I do not know –" '

'Look out!' cried Freddy.

Cecil entered from the garden. He was tall, with square shoulders, and he held his head high. Although he was well educated, rich and quite handsome, he still looked self conscious.

Mrs Honeychurch left her letter on the writing table.

'Oh, Cecil!' she exclaimed. 'Oh, Cecil, do tell me!'

'She has accepted me,' and he smiled with pleasure.

'I am so glad. Welcome to our family!' said Mrs Honeychurch, waving her hand at the furniture. 'I feel sure that you will make dear Lucy happy.'

'I hope so,' replied the young man, looking up at the ceiling. 'Lucy!' called out Cecil, because the conversation seemed to have stopped.

Lucy came across the grass, and smiled at them through the open door. Then she embraced her brother.

'Aren't you going to kiss me?' asked her mother.

Lucy kissed her also.

'Would you take them into the garden and tell Mrs Honeychurch all about it?' Cecil suggested. 'And I'll stay here and write to my mother.'

They went out into the sunlight. Smiling, Cecil lit a cigarette and reviewed the events that had led to such a happy conclusion.

He had known Lucy for several years, but only as an ordinary girl who was rather musical. He could still remember how depressed he had been that afternoon at Rome, when Lucy and her terrible cousin suddenly arrived and demanded to be taken to St Peter's Church. That day she had seemed like a typical tourist – speaking too loudly, dressed unattractively and exhausted by travel. But Italy changed her. It gave her light and – which was more precious to him – it gave her shadow. She did develop wonderfully day by day.

His feelings changed. He had felt superior at first. Now, slowly, although he did not feel passion, he was unsettled. He hinted that they might be suitable for each other. Her refusal had been clear and gentle; after it she behaved exactly the same as before. Three months later, in the Alps, he had asked her again. After her reply, he still did not feel rejected.

So now he had asked her once more, and, clear and gentle as ever, she had accepted him, giving him no reasons for her delay, but simply saying that she loved him and would do her best to make him happy. His mother, too, would be pleased; she had advised him what to do. He must write to her.

He sat down, and thought how the Windy Corner sitting room could be improved. The furniture was not really suitable. He thought about Freddy. 'He is only a boy – ' he reflected. 'I represent everything that he hates. Why should he want me for a brother-in-law?'

The Honeychurches were a respectable family, but he began to realise that Lucy was different; perhaps he ought to introduce her into more appropriate society as soon as possible.

'Mr Beebe!' said the maid, and the new vicar of Summer Street was shown in.

Cecil greeted him.

'I've come for tea and gossip, Mr Vyse. I met Sir Harry Otway as I came here. He has bought Cissie and Albert from Mr Flack!'

Cecil asked who Cissie and Albert were.

'You have been here a week and you do not know? Cissie and Albert are two villas that have been built opposite the church!'

'I am very stupid about local affairs,' said the young man, sounding bored. 'I only go into the country to see my friends and to enjoy the scenery.'

Mr Beebe was upset by Cecil's reaction to his news. He changed the subject. 'I forget, Mr Vyse – what is your profession?'

'I have no profession,' said Cecil. 'My attitude, which I cannot defend, is that as long as I am no trouble to anyone, I have a right to do as I like.'

'You are very fortunate,' said Mr Beebe. 'It is a wonderful opportunity, the possession of leisure.' His voice was a little disapproving; he had a regular occupation, and felt that others should have one also.

'I am glad that you approve.'

'Where are the others?' said Mr Beebe. 'I insist on having tea before the evening service.'

'I suppose Anne never told them you were here. In this house, one is told about the servants the day one arrives. The fault of Anne is that she kicks the chair-legs with her feet.'

'The fault of Mary is that she leaves brushes on the stairs.'

They both laughed, and things began to go better.

'The faults of Freddy – ' Cecil continued.

'Ah, he has too many. Try the faults of Miss Honeychurch.'

'She has none,' said the young man sincerely.

'I quite agree. At present she has none. I have a theory about Miss Honeychurch. Does it seem reasonable that she should play the piano so wonderfully, and live so quietly? I suspect that one day she will be wonderful in both. Music and life will mix.'

Cecil found his companion interesting. 'And at present you do not think her life is wonderful?'

'Since I came to Summer Street, she has been away. No, she wasn't wonderful in Florence, but I kept expecting that she would be. It was as if she had found wings, and meant to use them. I drew a picture with Miss Bartlett holding on to Lucy by a string.'

'The string has broken now.' Immediately Cecil realised that this was an inappropriate way of announcing their engagement, making him seem both proud and ridiculous. 'I mean,' he said, stiffly, 'she is going to marry me.'

The clergyman was conscious of some bitter disappointment which he could not keep out of his voice.

'I am sorry; I must apologise. I had no idea, or I would not have talked in this joking way.'

'I am sorry I have given you a shock,' Cecil said. 'I am afraid that you do not approve of Lucy's choice.'

'No, it's not that. But you ought to have stopped me.' He waved at the approaching group of people.

'Have you heard?' shouted Mrs Honeychurch, as she walked towards them. 'Oh, Mr Beebe, have you heard the news?'

'Yes, I have!' he cried. He looked at Lucy. 'Mrs Honeychurch, I am going to say what I am always supposed to say, but generally I am too shy. I want them all their lives to be good, and to be very happy as husband and wife, as father and mother. And now I want my tea.'

'You asked for your tea just in time. Stop being serious.'

Mr Beebe agreed. There were no more serious statements. And after the doubts of the afternoon, everyone then joined in a very pleasant tea party.

Chapter 7   Who Should Rent Cissie Villa?

A few days after the engagement was announced, Mrs Honeychurch made Lucy and Cecil come to a little garden party in the neighbourhood, because she wanted to show people that her daughter was going to marry a respectable man.

Cecil was more than respectable; he looked impressive, and it was very pleasant to see his elegant figure walking next to Lucy. People congratulated Mrs Honeychurch, and it pleased her.

At tea, there was an accident; a cup of coffee was spilt over Lucy's silk dress, and her mother took Lucy indoors so a maid could help her. They were gone for some time, and Cecil was left with the elderly guests. When they returned, he was not as pleasant as he had been.

'Do you go to this kind of party often?' he asked when they were driving home.

'Oh, now and then,' said Lucy, who had rather enjoyed herself.

'Is it typical of county society?'

'I suppose so.'

Cecil bent towards Lucy and said, 'I thought the congratulations were awful. It is so disgusting, the way an engagement is regarded as public property. All those old women smiling!'

'I suppose it's normal. They won't notice us so much next time.'

'But their attitude is wrong. An engagement is a private matter.'

'How annoying,' Lucy said. 'Couldn't you have escaped to play tennis?'

'I don't play tennis – at least, not in public. And I cannot help it if they do disapprove of me. There are certain barriers between myself and them, and I must accept them.'

'We all have our limits,' said Lucy wisely.

Cecil started to praise nature. He was not very familiar with the countryside, and occasionally got his facts wrong. 'I am a lucky person,' he finished. 'When I'm in London, I feel I could never live away from it. When I'm in the country, I feel the same about the country. I do believe that birds and trees and the sky are the most wonderful things in life, and that the people who live among them must be the best. It's true that most of them do not seem to notice anything. But both the country gentleman and the country labourer are more sympathetic to Nature than we are in the town. Do you feel that, Mrs Honeychurch?'

Mrs Honeychurch smiled. She had not been listening. Cecil felt annoyed, and decided not to say anything interesting again.

Lucy had not been listening either. Cecil quoted a line of poetry to her, and touched her knee with his own.

They arrived in Summer Street. There were pretty cottages and a stone church, but the scene was spoilt by two ugly little villas, Cissie and Albert. Albert was lived in. There were bright flowers in the garden, and curtains at the windows. Outside Cissie there was a noticeboard. The villa was available to rent.

'The place is ruined,' said the ladies, automatically. 'Summer Street will never be the same again.'

As the carriage passed, Cissie's door opened, and a gentleman came out.

'Stop!' cried Mrs Honeychurch. 'It's Sir Harry. Sir Harry, you must pull down these houses at once!'

Sir Harry Otway came to the carriage and said, 'Mrs Honeychurch, I meant to. But Miss Flack is living in Albert. What can I do. She is an old lady, and ill.'

'Ask her to leave,' said Cecil bravely.

Sir Harry sighed. He should have bought the land before the houses were built on it. After the building had started, he had realised how ugly the houses would be. The style was completely inappropriate for the neighbourhood. The builder refused to change the design, and it was only after the builder's aunt had moved into one of them that Sir Harry bought them both. He had failed in his duties to the countryside. He had spent money but Summer Street was still spoiled. All he could do now was to find someone respectable to rent Cissie – someone really suitable.

'The rent is ridiculously low,' he told them. 'But it is such a difficult size – too large for some people, too small for others.'

Cecil had been wondering whether he should despise the villas or despise Sir Harry for despising them. He decided on the latter. He waited for Sir Harry's reaction as he said, wickedly, 'You will find someone at once. I am sure that a bank clerk would think the house was wonderful.'

'Exactly!' said Sir Harry excitedly. 'I fear it will attract the wrong type of people.'

'Sir Harry,' said Lucy. 'I have an idea. How would you like older ladies?'

'My dear Lucy, it would be splendid. Do you know any?'

'Yes, I met them abroad. They are respectable and, at present, homeless. I heard from them last week. Miss Teresa and Miss Catharine Alan. I'm really not joking. They are the right kind of people. Mr Beebe knows them, too. May I tell them to write to you?'

'Indeed you may!' he cried.

'My advice,' said Mrs Honeychurch, 'is to have nothing to do with Lucy and her elderly ladies at all. It's a sad thing, but I would prefer to rent a house to someone for whom things are going well, than to someone who is having bad luck.'

'I understand what you are saying,' said Sir Harry, 'but it is, as you say, a very sad thing.'

'The Miss Alans aren't a sad thing!' cried Lucy.

'Yes, they are!' said Cecil. 'I haven't met them, but I should say they were a very unsuitable addition to the neighbourhood.'

'May I write to the Miss Alans?' Lucy asked Sir Harry.

'Please!' he cried. He invited Mrs Honeychurch to inspect Cissie.

Cecil said, 'Mrs Honeychurch, could we two walk home?'

'Certainly,' she replied.

Almost as soon as they could not be heard, Cecil said, 'Hopeless man!'

'Oh, Cecil. He isn't clever, but really he is nice.'

'No, Lucy; he represents everything that is wrong in country life. In London he would fit into his own level of society. But down here he behaves like a little god, looking important, and everyone – even your mother – is deceived by him.'

'All that you say is quite true,' said Lucy, although she felt depressed. 'I wonder whether it matters so very much?'

'It matters a lot. Oh, how cross I feel! I hope he gets some unsuitable person to rent that villa. Ugh! But let's forget him.'

Lucy was happy to do so. If Cecil disliked Sir Harry Otway, what guarantee was there that he would approve of the people who were important to her? For instance, Freddy. Freddy was neither clever nor beautiful, and so what would prevent Cecil saying, at any minute, 'I hate Freddy'? And what would she reply? She could only tell herself that Cecil had known Freddy for some time, and that they had always been pleasant to each other, except perhaps during the past few days.

'Which way shall we go?' she asked him.

'Are there two ways?'

'Perhaps the road is more sensible, as we're wearing smart clothes.'

'I'd rather go through the wood,' said Cecil. 'Why is it, Lucy, that you always say the road? Do you know that you have never once been with me in the fields or the wood since we were engaged?'

'Haven't I? The wood, then,' said Lucy, surprised by his strange comment.

She led the way into the wood, and he explained what he meant. 'I have got an idea – I may be wrong – that you feel more at home with me in a room.'

'A room?' she echoed, very puzzled.

'Yes. Or, at the most, in a garden, or on a road. Never in the real country, like this.'

'Oh, Cecil, what do you mean? I have never felt like that.'

'I connect you with a view – a certain type of view. Why shouldn't you connect me with a room?'

She reflected for a moment, and then said, laughing, 'Do you know that you're right? When I think of you, it's always in a room. How funny.'

To her surprise, he seemed annoyed.

'A sitting room? With no view?'

'Yes, with no view, I think. Why not?'

'I'd prefer you to connect me with the open air.'

She said again, 'Oh, Cecil, what do you mean?'

As there was no explanation, she led him further into the wood. They came to a shallow pool. She exclaimed, 'The Holy Lake!'

'Why do you call it that?'

'I can't remember why. I suppose it comes out of some book. It's small now, but you see that stream going through it? After it rains, the pool becomes quite large and beautiful. Freddy used to bathe there. He is very fond of it.'

Cecil looked at Lucy as she stood by the pool's edge. She reminded him of a brilliant flower.

'Lucy, I want to ask something of you that I have never asked before.'

At the serious note in his voice, she stepped kindly towards him.

'What, Cecil?'

'Until now – not even on the day you agreed to marry me –'

He became self-conscious and kept glancing round to see if they were observed. His courage had gone.

'Yes?'

'Until now I have never kissed you.'

Lucy went red.

'No – you haven't,' she murmured.

'Then – may I ask you now?'

'Of course you may, Cecil. You could have asked before.'

He was conscious of nothing sensible. As he approached her, he wished that he could change his mind. As he touched her, his gold eyeglass fell from his face.

He considered, after the embrace, that it had been a failure. Passion should not ask for permission. Why had he not done what any ordinary man would have done? He imagined the scene again. Lucy was standing flower-like by the water. He rushed up and took her in his arms. She at first refused to let him kiss her, then allowed him to, and admired him forever for his manly strength.

They left the pool in silence.

Chapter 8   Cecil's Unwelcome Involvement with Cissie Villa

The society in which Lucy moved was not very grand, but it was more grand than might have been expected. Her father, a wealthy local lawyer, had built Windy Corner to make some money at a time when people were moving into the district. He fell in love with the house, and in the end he lived there himself. Soon after his marriage, the social atmosphere began to alter. More houses were built. They were lived in by people who did not come from the district, but from London. They thought that the Honeychurches came from an upper-class background. Lucy's father was frightened by this, but his wife accepted the situation easily. 'It is extremely fortunate for the children,' she would say. She visited people, they visited her, and by the time people found out that her social background was not exactly the same as theirs they liked her, and it did not seem to matter. When Mr Honeychurch died, he had the satisfaction of leaving his family mixing with the very best society.

The best that was available. In fact, many of the inhabitants were rather dull, and Lucy realised this more clearly since her return from Italy. Until now she had accepted their ideals without question. Life was a group of rich, pleasant people, with exactly the same likes and dislikes. In this social group one thought, married and died. Outside it there was poverty and absence of style. But in Italy, things were different. She felt that there was no one whom she could not learn to like, that there were social barriers, but they were not particularly high. You could jump over them. She returned to England with new eyes.

Cecil saw things differently too, but Italy had made him not tolerant, but annoyed. He saw that the local society was narrow, but instead of saying, 'Does this matter very much?' he rebelled. He did not realise that Lucy concentrated on the positive areas of

49

her everyday life; although she was aware that her environment was not perfect, she refused to despise it totally. He did not realise something more important – that if she was too great for this society, she was too great for all society, and had reached the point where only personal relationships could satisfy her. She was a rebel, but not a rebel that he understood. She did not desire more variety; she desired to be equal with the man she loved, because Italy had offered her the most valuable of all possessions – her own soul.

◆

Lucy was playing a version of tennis with Minnie Beebe, the vicar's thirteen-year-old niece. She was trying to talk to Mr Beebe at the same time.

'Oh, it has been such a nuisance – first he, then they – no one knowing what they wanted.'

'But they are really coming now,' said Mr Beebe. 'I wrote to Miss Teresa Alan a few days ago – she was wondering how often the butcher called. They are coming. I heard from them this morning.'

'I shall hate those Miss Alans!' Mrs Honeychurch cried. 'Just because they are old and silly, one's expected to say, "How sweet!"'

Mr Beebe watched Lucy playing with Minnie. Cecil was absent – one did not play games when he was there.

Freddy joined them, interrupted the game, and managed to upset Minnie. Cecil heard the child crying from the house, and though he had some entertaining news, he did not come down to tell them, in case he got hurt. He was not a coward, but he hated the physical violence of the young.

'I wish the Miss Alans could see this,' observed Mr Beebe.

'Who are the Miss Alans?' Freddy asked.

'They have rented Cissie Villa.'

'That wasn't the name of the people that Sir Harry has rented it to.'

'Nonsense, Freddy! You know nothing about it,' said Lucy.

'Nonsense yourself! I've just seen him. He said to me that he had just found suitable people.'

'Exactly. The Miss Alans?'

'No. The name was more like Anderson.'

'Oh, dear, I hope there isn't going to be another muddle!' Mrs Honeychurch exclaimed.

'It's only another muddle of Freddy's,' answered Lucy. 'Freddy doesn't even know the name of the people he pretends have rented it instead.'

'Yes, I do. It's Emerson.'

'What name?'

'Emerson.'

'How Sir Harry does change his mind,' said Lucy quietly. 'I wish I had never bothered about it at all.'

Then she lay on her back and stared at the cloudless sky. Mr Beebe, whose good opinion of her increased every day, whispered to his niece that *that* was the proper way to behave if any little thing went wrong.

'I hope they are the right sort of person,' said Mrs Honeychurch. 'All right, Lucy,' – she was sitting up again – 'I can see what you are thinking. But there *is* a right sort and a wrong sort and it's silly to pretend there isn't.'

Freddy said, 'Well, you will be satisfied because they're friends of Cecil; so you and the other county families will be able to mix with them safely.'

'*Cecil?*' said Lucy.

'Friends of Cecil,' Freddy repeated, 'and so suitable.'

Lucy got up from the grass. It was difficult for her to learn that it was Cecil, not Sir Harry, who had been responsible for this. Mr Beebe was very sympathetic. He knew that Cecil took a wicked pleasure in upsetting people's plans. He looked at her kindly. When she exclaimed, 'But Cecil's Emersons – they can't possibly be the same ones – ' he took the opportunity of developing the conversation, so she could become calm. He said, 'The Emersons who were at Florence, do you mean? No, I don't suppose it will be them. Oh, Mrs Honeychurch, they were odd people! But we liked them, Lucy, didn't we? There was an incident with some violets. They picked violets and filled all the vases in the room where the Miss Alans were staying. Poor little ladies! So shocked and so pleased! Yes, I always connect those Emersons with violets.'

Lucy's face was very red. Mr Beebe saw this, and continued with his conversation. 'These Emersons consisted of a father and a son. People declared that the father had murdered his wife.'

Normally, Mr Beebe would never have repeated such gossip, but he was trying to help Lucy. He repeated any rubbish that came into his head.

'Murdered his wife?' said Mrs Honeychurch. 'Really, the Pension Bertolini must have been the oddest place. Whatever was Charlotte doing staying there? By the way, we really must ask Charlotte to stay some time.'

Lucy left them, still red with embarrassment. She was sure that talking to Cecil would calm her.

'Cecil!'

'Hello!' he called, and leant out of the smoking room window. He seemed in a very good mood. 'I was hoping you'd come. I have won a great victory. I have found people to rent the terrible Cissie Villa. Don't be angry! You'll forgive me when you hear the whole story.'

He looked very attractive when his face was bright, and her ridiculous doubts disappeared at once.

'I have heard,' she said. 'Freddy has told us. Naughty Cecil! I suppose I must forgive you. Just think of all the work I did for nothing. Certainly the Miss Alans are a little annoying, and I'd rather have nice friends of yours. But it isn't a joke.'

'Friends of mine?' he laughed. 'But Lucy, the best joke is this! Come here.' But she remained standing where she was. 'Do you know where I met these suitable people? In the National Gallery,★ when I went to London to see my mother last week.'

'What an odd place to meet people,' she said nervously. 'I don't quite understand.'

'In the Italian room. I'd never seen them before. However, we started talking. They had been to Italy.'

'But Cecil – '

He continued. 'During our conversation they said that they wanted a country cottage – the father to live in, the son to visit at weekends. I thought, "What a chance to make Sir Harry look silly!" I took their address, found out that they weren't criminals – it was great fun – and I wrote to him, saying – '

'Cecil! No, it's not fair. I've probably met them before – '

He ignored her 'It's perfectly fair. Anything is fair that punishes someone like Sir Harry. The old man will do this neighbourhood good. Sir Harry's views are disgusting. No, Lucy, different social classes should mix, and before long you'll agree with me. I believe in democracy – '

'No, you don't. You don't know what the word means.'

Cecil stared at Lucy. She looked very cross.

'It isn't fair, Cecil. I blame you – I blame you very much indeed. You should not have undone my arrangements concerning the Miss Alans and made me look ridiculous. You may think that you have made Sir Harry look silly, but what about how I look? I consider it most disloyal of you.'

She left him.

'Temper!' he thought, raising his eyebrows.

No, it was worse than temper. As long as Lucy had thought that his own smart friends were replacing the Miss Alans, she had

★National Gallery: an art gallery in London

not minded. He saw that these new people might be of educational value. He would tolerate the father, and get to know the son, who was silent. For reasons of both humour and Truth, he would bring them to Summer Street.

Chapter 9   An Unexpected Bathe Shocks the Ladies

The arrangements to bring the Emersons to Summer Street were completed easily. It was not a surprise that when Sir Harry Otway met Mr Emerson, he was disappointed. It was also not surprising that the Miss Alans were offended and wrote a letter to Lucy, whom they thought responsible for the failure. Mr Beebe planned pleasant moments for the newcomers, and told Mrs Honeychurch that Freddy must visit them as soon as they arrived.

Lucy at first felt desperate, but calmed down after deciding that it really did not matter. She was engaged now; the Emersons would not insult her, and they were welcome to come into the neighbourhood. And Cecil was welcome to introduce anyone he wanted into the neighbourhood. But it still remained a terrible event. She was glad that she was going to visit Mrs Vyse; the newcomers would move into Cissie Villa while she was safe in the London flat.

'Cecil – Cecil darling,' she whispered the evening she arrived, and crept into his arms.

'So you do love me, little thing?' he murmured.

'Oh, Cecil, I do! I don't know what I would do without you.'

Several days passed. Then she had a letter from Miss Bartlett. There was a coolness between the two cousins, and they had not written to each other since they parted in August. The coolness had started in Rome, where they had not got on well with each other.

The letter had been sent on from Windy Corner. In it, Charlotte said that Miss Lavish had been bicycling near Summer Street, and was astonished to see George Emerson come out from a house opposite the Church. He had told Miss Lavish that his father had rented the house. Charlotte begged Lucy to tell her family and Mr Vyse about his behaviour.

Lucy was very annoyed by the letter, and replied that she had promised Charlotte that she would never tell her mother. She had kept her promise and could not possibly tell her mother now. She had said both to her mother and Cecil that she had met the Emersons in Florence.

In fact, Lucy had tried to tell Cecil about George Emerson when they were laughing about some beautiful lady that he had fallen in love with when he was at school. But her body had behaved so ridiculously that she stopped.

She and her secret stayed ten days longer in London. Much of London society was on holiday, but despite the absence of so many people, Mrs Vyse managed to organise a dinner party consisting entirely of the grandchildren of famous people. Lucy was impressed. Everyone appeared tired of everything. They talked about enthusiasms which they had then abandoned. In this atmosphere the Pension Bertolini and Windy Corner appeared equally unpolished. Lucy realised that her London career would separate her a little from everything that she had loved in the past.

The grandchildren asked her to play the piano. She played Schumann. When the guests had left and Lucy had gone to bed, Mrs Vyse discussed the little party with her son.

'Lucy is becoming a wonderful person,' she said. 'She is becoming less like the Honeychurches and more like us. The Honeychurches are excellent people, but you know what I mean. She is not always talking about servants or cooking.'

'Italy has done it,' said Cecil.

'Perhaps,' Mrs Vyse murmured.

As she was going to sleep, she heard a cry from Lucy's room. She found the girl sitting upright with her hand on her cheek.

'I am so sorry, Mrs Vyse – it is these dreams.'

The older lady smiled and kissed her, saying very distinctly, 'You should have heard us talking about you, dear. He admires you more than ever. Dream of that.'

◆

It was a bright Saturday afternoon in autumn, after heavy rain. Mr Beebe leant over his vicarage gate. Freddy leant next to him, smoking a pipe.

'Let's go and bother those new people opposite for a little. They might amuse you,' suggested Mr Beebe.

Freddy said that the new people might be a bit busy, since they had only just moved in.

'I think we should bother them.' They went across the grass towards Cissie Villa. 'Hello!' Mr Beebe called, shouting through the open door, through which they could see a mess.

A serious voice replied, 'Hello.'

'I've brought someone to see you.'

'I'll be down in a minute.'

The passage was blocked by a wardrobe. Mr Beebe went round it with difficulty. The sitting room itself was blocked with books.

'Mr Beebe, look at that,' Freddy said. On the top of the wardrobe someone had painted a quotation: 'Distrust all events that require new clothes.'

'I know, isn't it fun?' replied Mr Beebe. 'I like that. I'm certain that the old man did it.'

But Freddy was his mother's son, and thought that one ought not to spoil the furniture.

'Did Miss Honeychurch enjoy London?' asked the vicar.

'Yes, very much,' said Freddy, picking up a book. 'She and Cecil are closer than ever. Oh, I wish I wasn't such a fool, Mr Beebe. Lucy used to be nearly as stupid as I am, but it'll be very different now, Mother thinks. She will read all kinds of books.'

'So will you.'

'Only medical books. Not books that you can talk about afterwards.'

George Emerson ran downstairs and joined them in the room.

'Let me introduce Mr Honeychurch, a neighbour,' said Mr Beebe.

Then Freddy said for no clear reason, 'How do you do? Come and have a bathe.'

'Oh, all right,' answered George, with no expression. Old Mr Emerson came slowly down the stairs.

'Good afternoon, Mr Beebe. These two young people are going to be friends.'

'Let me introduce Mr Honeychurch, whose sister you will remember from Florence,' said Mr Beebe.

'How do you do?' said Mr Emerson. 'I'm very glad to see you, and that you are taking George for a bathe. I'm also very glad that your sister is going to marry. Marriage is a duty. I am sure that she will be happy, because we know Mr Vyse, too. He has been most kind. He met us by chance in the National Gallery and arranged everything about this delightful house. Though I hope Sir Harry Otway is not angry. I spoke to him about his attitude to the laws on hunting. Anyway, go and bathe, George, and then bring everyone back for tea.'

Mr Beebe felt he ought to help Freddy, and led the way out of the house and into the woods. He did not like silence, and felt he must keep talking, since the expedition looked like a failure, and neither of his companions would utter a word. He spoke about Florence. 'And how odd that you should meet Mr Vyse! Did you realise that you would find all the inhabitants of the Pension Bertolini here?'

'I did not. Miss Lavish told me,' replied George.

'Things don't happen by chance very often,' said Mr Beebe. 'It isn't just by chance that you are here now, when you reflect on it.'

To his relief, George began to talk.

'It is. I have reflected. It is fate. Everything is fate. We are brought together by fate, and driven apart by fate.'

'You have not reflected at all,' answered the clergyman. 'Where did you first meet Miss Honeychurch and myself?'

'In Italy.'

'And where did you meet Mr Vyse, who is going to marry Miss Honeychurch?'

'National Gallery.'

'Looking at Italian art. You want to find Italian things, and so do we and our friends. And so we meet again.'

'It is fate that I am here,' insisted George. 'But you can call it Italy if it makes you less unhappy.'

Mr Beebe wanted to move the conversation on. 'We are all so glad that you have come here.'

Silence.

'Here we are!' called Freddy.

'Oh, good!' exclaimed Mr Beebe, wiping his forehead.

They climbed down a slippery bank. There was the pool. It was small, but after the rain the waters had flooded the surrounding grass. It was very green, and made the pool look inviting.

George sat down where the grass was dry, and began to take off his boots. He looked bored.

'I love these plants,' said Mr Beebe. 'What is the name of this one?'

No one knew or seemed to care.

'Mr Beebe, aren't you bathing?' called Freddy, as he undressed.

Mr Beebe thought he was not.

'The water's wonderful,' cried Freddy, as he ran in.

'Water's water,' murmured George. Wetting his hair first, he followed Freddy towards the water, showing no emotion.

Freddy swam a little way before becoming stuck in mud. He changed direction, and met mud again.

'Is it worth it?' asked George. The bank broke away, and he fell into the pool.

'Ugh, I've swallowed something. Mr Beebe, the water's wonderful, absolutely wonderful. Come in,' invited Freddy.

'The water's quite nice,' said George.

Mr Beebe, who was hot, and always joined in where possible, looked around him. He could see no one from his parish, only trees against the blue sky. How marvellous it was!

'I suppose I can wash too.' Soon his clothes were in a third little pile on the bank, and he too entered the water.

It was ordinary water, and there was not very much of it, and, as Freddy said, it reminded one of swimming in a salad. The three gentlemen swam around the pool. But either because of the sun, or because two of the gentlemen were young in years, and the third young in his attitude towards life, they forgot everything and began to play. Mr Beebe and Freddy splashed each other. A little respectfully, they splashed George. He was quiet, they feared that they had offended him. Then suddenly, he smiled. He threw himself at them, splashed them, kicked them, muddied them, and chased them out of the pool.

'I'll race you around it, then,' cried Freddy, and they raced in the sunshine. Then Mr Beebe agreed to run – an unforgettable sight.

They ran to get dry, they bathed to get cool, they played in the bushes, they bathed to get clean. They played with the piles of clothes.

'Goal!'

'Goal!'

'Be careful of my watch!' cried Mr Beebe.

Clothes flew in all directions.

'Be careful of my hat! No, that's enough, Freddy. Get dressed now.'

But the two young men were in another world. They ran into the trees. Freddy carried Mr Beebe's shirt under his arm, George was wearing Mr Beebe's hat on his wet hair.

'That's enough,' shouted Mr Beebe, remembering that, after all, he was in his own parish. 'Stop! I can see people coming. *Ladies*!'

Neither George nor Freddy heard Mr Beebe's last warning, or they would have avoided Mrs Honeychurch, Cecil and Lucy, who were walking through the wood to visit Mrs Butterworth, an elderly neighbour. Freddy dropped Mr Beebe's shirt at their feet, and ran into the bushes. George turned and ran towards the pool, still wearing Mr Beebe's hat.

'Goodness!' cried Mrs Honeychurch. 'Whoever were these unfortunate people? Oh, dears, don't look! And poor Mr Beebe, too! Whatever has happened?'

'Come this way immediately,' commanded Cecil, who always felt he must lead women, though he did not know where, and protect them, though he did not know against what. He led them now towards the bushes where Freddy was hiding.

'Oh, poor Mr Beebe! Was that his shirt we left in the path? Cecil, Mr Beebe's shirt – '

'I think Mr Beebe jumped back into the pool.'

'This way, please, Mrs Honeychurch, this way.' They followed Cecil up the bank.

'Well, *I* can't help it,' said a voice. Freddy appeared in front of them.

'So it's you, dear! Why not have a comfortable bath at home with hot and cold water?' Mrs Honeychurch asked her son. 'Come, Lucy.' They turned. 'Oh look – don't look! Oh, poor Mr Beebe! How unfortunate again – '

Mr Beebe was just crawling out of the pool. Underwear was floating on the surface.

'Mother, do come away,' cried Lucy. 'Oh, do come.'

'Hello,' cried George, so that again the ladies stopped.

He was half-dressed. Barefoot and bare-chested, he called, 'Hello, Miss Honeychurch! Hello!'

'Bow, Lucy, you must bow. Whoever is it? I shall bow.'

Lucy obeyed her mother, and bowed.

Chapter 10   Charlotte Bartlett Comes to Stay

While at tea with Mrs Butterworth, Lucy thought about her meeting with George. It had not been as she had imagined it. She had thought he might be shy or cold or even impolite. She was prepared for that. But she had not imagined that he would be happy, and greet her cheerfully.

The tea party was to celebrate the engagement. Mrs Butterworth had wanted to meet Cecil, but Cecil did not want to listen to Mrs Butterworth talking about gardens. When he was cross, he always gave long, clever answers to questions, instead of saying 'yes' or 'no'. Lucy joined in the conversation a little, to try and keep Cecil cheerful.

'Lucy,' said her mother, when they got home, 'is anything wrong with Cecil?'

'No, I don't think so, Mother. Cecil's all right.'

'Perhaps he's tired. Because otherwise, I cannot explain his behaviour.'

'I do think Mrs Butterworth is a little annoying, if that is what you mean.'

'Cecil has told you to think so.'

'Cecil has a very high standard for people,' said Lucy, seeing that this conversation was going to be difficult. 'It's part of his ideals – '

'Oh, rubbish! If high ideals make a young man rude, then he should get rid of them as soon as he can,' said Mrs Honeychurch.

'I never told you – I had a letter from Charlotte while I was away in London.'

Mrs Honeychurch did not like Lucy's attempt to change the subject. She continued, 'Since Cecil came back from London, nothing seems to please him. When I speak, he winces. I know that I am not an intellectual; I don't know a great deal about art, or literature or music. I realise he dislikes the sitting room furniture, but your father bought it, and we must live with it. Please could Cecil kindly remember that.'

'I – I see what you mean, and Cecil oughtn't to behave like that. But he does not mean to be impolite – he once explained – it is the *things* that upset him – he is easily upset by ugly things – he is not impolite to *people*.'

Lucy found it harder to explain Cecil's behaviour in her own home than when she was in London. There was no doubt that Cecil had meant to be superior, and had succeeded. And Lucy – she did not know why – wished that this trouble could have come at another time.

Going upstairs to change for dinner, Lucy sighed to herself, 'Oh dear, what shall I do, what shall I do?' Then Freddy came running up the stairs.

'Lucy, the Emersons are great people. I want to ask them to tennis next week on Sunday.'

'Oh, I wouldn't do that, Freddy,' said Lucy. 'It's better not to. I really mean it.'

Mrs Honeychurch opened her bedroom door.

'Lucy, did you say you had had a letter from Charlotte?'

'Yes.'

'Did she mention the builders?' Mrs Honeychurch asked.

'The *what*?'

'Don't you remember that she was going to have builders in her house in October, and her water tank replaced, and the pipes cleaned. All sorts of terrible things.'

'I can't remember all Charlotte's worries,' said Lucy bitterly. 'I shall have enough worries of my own, now that you are not pleased with Cecil.'

Mrs Honeychurch might have got angry. She did not. 'Come here, dear, and kiss me.' And though nothing is perfect, Lucy felt that for the moment her mother and Windy Corner were perfect.

At dinner, Mrs Honeychurch asked, 'Lucy, how well did you know the Emersons at the Bertolini?'

'Oh, not very well. Charlotte knew them even less well.'

'That reminds me – you never told me what Charlotte said in her letter to you,' said Mrs Honeychurch.

'A number of things,' replied Lucy, wondering if she would be able to sit through dinner without telling a lie.

'Did she say how she was? Did she sound cheerful? I have been thinking. I know that Charlotte will have builders in her house next week. She could come here, and we could give her a nice holiday. I have not seen poor Charlotte for a long time.'

'Mother, no!' Lucy begged. 'It's impossible. Freddy has a friend coming on Tuesday, Cecil is here, Minnie Beebe is coming to stay as well. It isn't fair on the maids to have so many guests.'

'The truth is, dear, you don't like Charlotte.'

'No, I don't. And Cecil doesn't either. You haven't seen her recently, and don't realise how annoying she can be, even though she is a good person.'

'I agree,' said Cecil.

Mrs Honeychurch, sounding more serious than usual, replied, 'Neither of you is being very kind. You have each other, and these beautiful woods to walk in. Charlotte has the builders in her house, and no water. You are young, dears, and however clever young people are, and however many books they read, they will never guess what it feels like to grow old.'

'I can't help it, Mother. I don't like Charlotte. I admit it's horrible of me.'

'From what you've said, it seems you almost told her so,' said her mother.

'Well, she made us leave Florence so quickly – ' The ghosts of Lucy's past were returning. The Holy Lake would never be the same. And next Sunday, something would happen at Windy Corner. How could she fight these ghosts?

◆

Of course, Miss Bartlett accepted the invitation. She was sure she would be a nuisance. She begged to be given an inferior guest room – a room with no view. She sent her love to Lucy.

George Emerson accepted the invitation to tennis on Sunday. Lucy faced the situation bravely. When she imagined strange things, she explained it by telling herself it was due to her nerves. She was nervous at night. When she talked to George – they met again almost immediately at the vicarage – his voice affected her deeply, and she wished to remain near him. How awful if she really wished to remain near him! Of course, the wish was due to nerves.

In spite of very clear directions, Miss Bartlett managed to make a muddle of her arrival. She was supposed to arrive at the southeastern station at Dorking, and Mrs Honeychurch drove to meet her. She arrived at another station, where there was no one to meet her, so she had to take a cab. When she arrived at Windy Corner, there was no one there except Freddy and his friend, Mr Floyd, who had to stop playing tennis, and entertain her for a whole hour. At four o'clock Lucy and Cecil arrived, with Minnie Beebe, and they all had tea in the garden.

'I shall never forgive myself,' said Miss Bartlett. 'I have upset everything. Disturbing young people. But I insist on paying for my cab. Please let me do that.'

In the end, Lucy agreed. But Miss Bartlett had no change. Could anyone give her change?

A discussion followed. Everyone joined in. Freddy had some change, so did his friend. Freddy owed Cecil money, so Miss Bartlett could give her money directly to him, since Freddy had paid for the cab. Miss Bartlett, who was not good at mathematics, got in a muddle. Minnie Beebe objected to the solution. She was given cake, but would not stop talking about it. Finally, Lucy got up.

'I'll get some change from one of the maids, and we'll start again from the beginning.'

'Lucy, what a nuisance I am,' protested Miss Bartlett, and followed her across the grass. When they could not be heard, Miss Bartlett said, 'Have you told him about him yet?'

'No, I haven't,' replied Lucy, and was then cross with herself for understanding so quickly what her cousin meant. She escaped from Charlotte into the kitchen.

'I haven't told Cecil or anyone,' she remarked, when she returned. 'I promised you I wouldn't. Here is your money. Will you count it?'

Miss Bartlett was in the sitting room, staring at a painting.

'How awful,' murmured Charlotte. 'How awful it would be if Mr Vyse heard about it from some other source.'

'Oh no, Charlotte,' said Lucy. 'George Emerson is all right, and what other source is there?'

Miss Bartlett considered. 'For example, the driver. I saw him looking through the bushes at you. I remember he had a violet between his teeth.'

Lucy trembled a little. 'How could a Florentine cab driver ever contact Cecil?'

'We must think of every possibility. Perhaps old Mr Emerson knows. In fact, he is certain to know.'

'I don't care if he does. I was grateful to you for your letter, but even if the news does get round, I think I can trust Cecil to laugh at it.' However, in her heart she knew that she could not trust him to laugh at it, because he did not want her to have been touched by another man.

'Very well, dear,' said Charlotte. 'You know best. Perhaps gentlemen are different now than when I was young. Ladies are certainly different.'

'Charlotte!' Lucy struck at her playfully. 'You kind, anxious thing! What *would* you like me to do? First you say, "Don't tell", and then you say, "Tell". Which should it be?'

Miss Bartlett sighed. 'I am not as good as you at conversation, dear. I feel ashamed when I think how I got involved with everything at Florence, and you were so able to look after yourself, and so much cleverer in all ways than I am. You will never forgive me.'

'Shall we go out, then?'

'Dear, one moment,' said Miss Bartlett. 'We may not have this chance for a chat again. Have you seen the young man yet?'

'Yes, I have.'

'What happened?'

'We met at the vicarage.'

'What is he saying about it?'

'Nothing. He talked about Italy, like any other person. It really is all right. What advantage would he get from behaving like a cad? I do wish I could make you see it my way. He really won't be any nuisance, Charlotte.'

'Once a cad, always a cad. That is my poor opinion.'

Lucy paused. 'Cecil said one day – and I thought it was clever – that there are two kinds of cad – the conscious and the subconscious.' She paused again, wanting to represent Cecil's opinion accurately. Through the window she saw Cecil turning over the pages of a novel. It was a new one from the library. Her mother must have returned from the station.

'Once a cad, always a cad,' repeated Miss Bartlett.

'What I mean by subconscious is that Mr Emerson lost his head. I fell into all those violets, and he was silly and surprised. I don't think we ought to blame him very much. It makes such a difference when you see a person with beautiful things behind him unexpectedly. It really does; it makes an enormous difference. He doesn't admire me or any of that nonsense. Freddy rather likes him and has asked him up here on Sunday, so you can judge for yourself. He has improved. He doesn't always look at if he is going to burst into tears. He is a clerk in the General Manager's office at one of the big railways – not a porter! – and comes to visit his father at weekends. His father was a journalist, but is retired. Now let's go into the garden.' She took Charlotte by the arm. 'Let's not talk about this silly Italian business any more. We want you to have a nice relaxing visit at Windy Corner, with no worrying.'

Lucy thought that this was rather a good speech. There was one unfortunate mistake in it. It cannot be said if Miss Bartlett noticed it, because it is impossible to understand how elderly people think.

Just then Mrs Honeychurch interrupted them. There were explanations about Charlotte's journey, and in the middle of them Lucy escaped, memories beating in her brain.

Chapter 11   The Disaster of Cecil's Library Book

The Sunday after Miss Bartlett's arrival was a wonderful day, like most of the days of that year. The garden of Windy Corner was deserted except for a red book, which lay on the garden path. From the house came sounds of females preparing themselves for church. 'The men say they won't go.' – 'Well, I don't blame them.' – 'Minnie says, need she go?' – 'Tell her, no nonsense.'

Lucy stepped outside. Her new red dress did not suit her. She was wearing an engagement ring.

'Lucy! Lucy! What's that book? Who's been taking a book off the shelf and leaving it outside to spoil?'

'It's only the library book that Cecil's been reading.'

'Pick it up,' ordered her mother.

Lucy picked up the book and glanced at the title: *In a Piazza*. She no longer read novels herself. She spent all her free time reading serious literature, hoping to catch up with Cecil. It was awful how little she knew, and even when she thought she knew something, like the Italian painters, she found she had forgotten it. This morning she had confused two painters with similar names, and Cecil had said, 'What! You aren't forgetting Italy already?'

'Lucy – have you some money for Minnie and yourself?'

Lucy ran to her mother, who was worrying about the preparations for church.

'Minnie, don't be late. Here comes the carriage. Where's Charlotte? Why *is* she taking so much time? Poor Charlotte! Minnie!'

Minnie was protesting. She did not want to go to church. Why shouldn't she sit in the sun with the young men? Miss Bartlett, dressed very fashionably, came slowly down the stairs.

'How smart you look,' said Mrs Honeychurch.

'If I did not wear my best clothes now, when should I wear them?' asked Charlotte, and got into the carriage.

'Goodbye! Be good!' called Cecil. He sounded superior. His opinions about religion upset Lucy.

She saw the Emersons after church. There was a line of carriages outside, and the Honeychurch carriage was opposite Cissie Villa. The Emersons were in the garden.

'Introduce me,' said her mother. 'Unless the young man considers that he knows me already.'

He probably did, but Lucy ignored the Holy Lake and introduced them formally. Old Mr Emerson said he was glad that she was going to be married. She said yes, she was glad too; and then, as Miss Bartlett and Minnie were behind her with Mr Beebe, she changed the conversation to a less disturbing topic, and asked him how he liked his new house.

'Very much,' he replied, but he sounded offended. He had never sounded offended before. He added, 'We have just found out that the Miss Alans were coming to this house, before we were offered it. Women mind things like that. I am very upset about it.'

'I believe that there was some confusion,' said Mrs Honeychurch, a little nervously.

'I wonder whether we ought to write to the Miss Alans and offer to give it back to them. What do you think?' He appealed to Lucy.

'Oh, you must stay now you have come,' said Lucy, lightly. She must avoid criticising Cecil, who was responsible for this incident.

'Freddy is looking forward to seeing you this afternoon,' said Mrs Honeychurch. 'Do you play tennis? Mr Emerson, if you could come with your son we would be so pleased.'

He thanked her, but said the walk sounded a little too far for him.

Miss Bartlett approached.

'You know our cousin, Miss Bartlett,' said Mrs Honeychurch pleasantly. 'You met her with my daughter in Florence.'

'Yes, indeed!' said the old man, starting to walk towards Miss Bartlett to greet her. Miss Bartlett immediately got into the carriage. From inside, she made a formal bow. It was just like the Pension Bertolini again. It was the old, old battle of the room with a view.

George did not respond to the bow. Like any boy, he went red and was ashamed; he knew that the chaperone remembered. He said, 'I – I'll come up to tennis later, if I can,' and went into the house. His clumsy behaviour affected Lucy. Men were not in fact gods, but as human and as clumsy as girls; even men might suffer from unexplained desires, and need help. To someone of Lucy's background, this discovery that men could be weak was significant, but she had first noticed it in Florence when George threw her photographs into the river.

'George, don't go!' cried his father. 'George has been so cheerful today. I am sure he will come this afternoon.'

'Yes,' said Lucy, ignoring the expression on Charlotte's face, and speaking loudly. 'I do hope he will.'

Then she went to the carriage and murmured to Charlotte, 'The old man hasn't been told; I knew it was all right.' Mrs Honeychurch followed her, and they drove away.

Lucy was full of joy on the way home. 'He has not told, he has not told.' She longed to shout the words. 'It's a secret between the two of us for ever. Cecil will never hear about it.' The secret was safe. Only three English people knew about it in the world.

She greeted Cecil enthusiastically, because she felt so safe. As he helped her out of the carriage, she said, 'The Emersons have been so nice. George Emerson has improved enormously.'

'Oh, how are my pupils?' asked Cecil, who was no longer interested in them. He had forgotten that he had decided to bring them to Windy Corner for educational purposes.

'Pupils!' she said.

The only relationship that Cecil understood was one of protector and protected. He had no idea of the companionship that Lucy desired.

'You can see for yourself how your pupils are. George Emerson is coming here this afternoon. He is a most interesting man to talk to. But don't – ' She nearly said, 'Don't protect him.' But it was lunchtime and, as often happened, Cecil was not paying attention to her remarks.

Lunch was a cheerful meal. Lucy felt she had received a guarantee. Her mother would always sit in her place, her brother in his. The sun would never be hidden behind the hills.

After lunch, they asked her to play the piano. Just as she had finished, George arrived. She went very red, and started playing the piano again. She played badly, and then stopped.

'I vote we play tennis,' said Freddy.

'Why don't you four men play?'

'Not for me, thank you,' said Cecil. 'I don't want to spoil the game.'

'Oh, come along, Cecil. I don't play well, neither does Floyd and I expect George plays badly as well,' said Freddy.

George corrected him. 'I don't play badly.'

'Then certainly I won't play,' said Cecil.

'Then it will have to be Lucy,' said Mrs Honeychurch. 'Lucy, go and change your clothes.'

Mr Floyd was her tennis partner. She liked music, but how much better tennis seemed. She was surprised that George seemed very anxious to win the game. She remembered how he was in Florence. Leaning against the wall, he had said to her, 'I shall want to live.' He wanted to live now, to win at tennis; and he did win.

The countryside around them looked beautiful. She might be forgetting some things about Italy, but she was noticing more things about England. How beautiful the view was!

But now Cecil wanted her attention. He had been rather a nuisance during the tennis. The novel he was reading was so bad that he read it aloud to the others. He wandered around the tennis court and called out, 'Listen to this, Lucy.'

'Awful!' said Lucy, and missed the ball. When they had finished the game, he still continued reading; there was a murder scene, and he wanted everyone to listen to it. Freddy and Mr Floyd had to look for a lost tennis ball in the bushes, but George and Lucy listened.

'The scene starts in Florence.'

'What fun! Cecil, go on reading. Come, Mr Emerson, sit down after all your energy,' invited Lucy.

He jumped over the tennis net, and sat down at her feet, asking, 'You – and are you tired?'

'Of course I'm not!'

'The scene starts in Florence,' repeated Cecil. ' "Sunset. Leonora was hurrying – " '

Lucy interrupted. 'Leonora? Is Leonora the heroine? Who's written the book?'

'Joseph Emery Prank. "Sunset. Leonora was hurrying across the square. She was praying to the saints that she would not arrive too late. Sunset – the sunset of Italy. At the edge of the square – " '

Lucy started laughing. ' "Joseph Emery Prank"! It's Miss Lavish! It's Miss Lavish's novel, and she has published it using someone else's name.'

'Who is Miss Lavish?' asked Cecil.

'Oh, an awful person – Mr Emerson, you remember Miss Lavish?'

George looked up. 'Of course I do. I saw her the day I arrived at Summer Street. It was she who told me that you lived here.'

'It is not surprising that the novel's bad,' Lucy continued. 'I never liked Miss Lavish. But I suppose we ought to read the book, as we've met her.'

'All modern books are bad,' said Cecil, who was annoyed that she was not paying attention. 'Everyone writes for money these days.'

'Oh, Cecil!'

'It's true. I will stop forcing you to listen to Joseph Emery Prank.'

Cecil, this afternoon, seemed ridiculous. Leaving him to be annoyed, she stared at George's black head, which was almost touching her knee. She did not want to stroke it, but she saw herself wanting to stroke it; it was a curious sensation.

'How do you like this view of ours, Mr Emerson?'

'My father – ' He looked up at her (and he was a little red) – 'says that there is only one perfect view – the view of the sky straight over our heads — and that all these views on earth are bad copies of it. He told us that views are really crowds — crowds of trees and houses and hills — and they look like each other, like human crowds. They have a mysterious power over us.'

Lucy's lips opened.

George continued. 'A crowd is more than the people who are in it. Something gets added to it — no one knows how — just as something has got added to those hills.'

'What a splendid idea!' she murmured. 'I shall enjoy hearing your father talk again.'

'There's a ridiculous account of a view in this book,' said Cecil.

'Mr Emerson, have you any brothers or sisters?' asked Lucy.

Cecil closed the book with a bang. 'I will stop forcing you to listen to Joseph Emery Prank.' He got up. He was going to walk away, but Lucy stopped him.

'Cecil, do read the thing about the view.'

He sat down again. 'Chapter two,' he said, yawning. 'Find me chapter two, if it's not too much trouble.'

She found chapter two, and glanced at its opening sentences. She thought she had gone mad.

'Here — hand me the book.'

She heard her voice saying, 'It isn't worth reading — it's too silly to read — I never saw such rubbish. It oughtn't to have been published.'

Cecil took the book from her.

' "Leonora sat sad and alone. In front of her was the Italian countryside. It was spring. Far away were the towers of Florence, while the bank she sat on was covered in violets. Unseen, Antonio crept up behind her — " '

So Cecil would not see her face, Lucy turned to George, and saw his face.

Cecil continued, ' "He spoke no words. He simply embraced her in his manly arms." '

73

There was a silence.

'This isn't the part I wanted,' Cecil informed them. 'There is a much funnier part, later in the book.' He turned the pages.

'Shall we go in to tea?' Lucy's voice remained steady.

She led the way through the garden. She thought a disaster had been prevented. But Cecil had forgotten the book, and returned to fetch it. George, who loved passionately, knocked into her on the narrow path.

'No – ' she said, and, for the second time, was kissed by him.

As if no more was possible, he left her. Cecil returned; they walked across the grass alone.

Chapter 12   Lucy Lies to George and Cecil

Lucy had developed since the spring. She was better at hiding her emotions. There were no tears. She said to Cecil, 'I am not coming in to tea – tell Mother – I must write some letters,' and went up to her room. There she prepared for action.

She sent for Miss Bartlett.

Lucy's first aim was to defeat her feelings. She forgot the truth. She remembered that she was engaged to Cecil; she forced herself to confuse her memories of George. He meant nothing to her; he had never meant anything to her. He had behaved very badly; she had never encouraged him. In a few moments, Lucy was ready for battle.

'Something awful has happened,' she began, as soon as her cousin arrived. 'Do you know anything about Miss Lavish's novel?'

Miss Bartlett looked surprised, and said that she had not read the book, nor known that it was published.

'There is a love scene in it. The hero and heroine are on a hillside, and Florence is in the distance.'

'Lucy, dear, I am completely confused. I know nothing at all about it.'

'There are violets. I cannot believe that this has happened by chance. Charlotte, Charlotte, how *could* you have told her? It *must* be you.'

'Told her what?' Charlotte asked, becoming more anxious.

'About that awful afternoon in February.'

Miss Bartlett was genuinely upset. 'Oh, Lucy, dearest girl – she hasn't put that in her book?'

Lucy nodded.

'And can it be recognised?'

'Yes.'

'Then Eleanor Lavish will never – never – never more be my friend.'

'So you did tell?'

'I did mention – when I had tea with her in Rome – '

'But, Charlotte, what about the promise? Why did you tell Miss Lavish, when you wouldn't even let me tell Mother?'

'I will never forgive Eleanor. She has betrayed my trust.'

'Why did you tell her, though? This is a most serious thing.'

Why does anyone tell anything? Miss Bartlett only sighed in response. She had done wrong. She admitted it.

Lucy stamped her foot on the ground angrily. 'Cecil read the part of the book aloud to me and to Mr Emerson; it upset Mr Emerson, and he insulted me again. When Cecil was not looking. Ugh! Is it possible that men are such animals?'

Miss Bartlett was full of regrets. 'Oh, Lucy – I shall never forgive myself, never until I die.'

'I see now why you wanted me to tell Cecil, and what you meant by "some other source". You knew that you had told Miss Lavish, and that she was not reliable.' Miss Bartlett winced. 'However, we cannot do anything about it now,' continued Lucy. 'I am in a very difficult situation. How can I get out of it?'

Miss Bartlett could not think. The days of her energy were over. She was a visitor, not a chaperone. She stood still, while Lucy got more and more angry.

'I think I shall go mad. I have no one to help me. What *does* a girl do when she meets a cad? We've both made a muddle of it. George Emerson is still in the garden. Will he be punished, or won't he? I want to know.'

Charlotte felt helpless. She moved towards the window.

'Could you speak to him again now?' demanded Lucy.

'Eleanor Lavish will never again be my friend.'

'Yes or no, please; yes or no.'

'It is the kind of thing that only a gentleman is able to settle.'

'Very well,' said Lucy, with an angry gesture. 'No one will help me. I will speak to him myself.' And immediately she realised that this was what her cousin had intended the whole time.

George Emerson was coming up the garden with a tennis ball in his hand.

Lucy's anger faded when she saw him. She said to Charlotte, 'Freddy has taken him to the dining room for tea. The others are going into the garden. Come with me. I want you in the room with me, of course.'

They went downstairs, and into the dining room. 'Try the jam,' Freddy was saying. 'The jam's very good.'

'Freddy, you go and join the others,' said Lucy. 'Charlotte and I will give Mr Emerson his tea.'

Freddy went outside, singing.

Lucy sat down at the table. Miss Bartlett, who was very frightened, picked up a book and pretended to read.

Lucy said, 'Mr Emerson, I cannot even talk to you. Go out of this house, and never come into it again as long as I live here.' She pointed at the door. 'I hate arguments. Go, please.'

'You don't mean,' George said, absolutely ignoring Miss Bartlett, 'you don't mean that you are going to marry that man.'

'You are quite ridiculous,' she said quietly.

Then he spoke seriously. 'You cannot live with Vyse. He should never have a close relationship with anyone, especially not a woman.'

She had never thought about Cecil like that.

'Have you ever talked to Vyse without feeling tired? He is the sort of person who is all right as long as he concentrates on things – books, pictures – but hopeless when he spends time with people. That's why I am speaking to you in all this muddle, even now. It's shocking enough for me to lose you, but sometimes a man has to deny himself joy. I would have done nothing if your Cecil had been a different person. But I saw him first at the National Gallery, where he winced because my father mispronounced the names of famous painters. Then he brings us here to play a silly trick on a kind neighbour. Next I meet you together, and find him protecting you and teaching you and your mother to be shocked about things, when that should be your decision. Cecil doesn't dare let a woman decide. He's the type that has kept Europe in the past for a thousand years. Every moment of his life he's forming you, telling you what is charming or amusing or ladylike. And you, you of all women, listen to his voice instead of to your own. The book made me kiss you, and I wish I had controlled myself. I'm not ashamed. I won't apologise. But it has frightened you, and you may not have noticed that I love you.'

'You say that Mr Vyse wants me to listen to him, Mr Emerson,' said Lucy. 'It seems that you have the same habit.'

George answered, 'Yes, I have,' and sat down as if suddenly tired. 'But I do love you – surely in a better way than he does.' He thought, 'Yes – really in a better way. I want you to have your own thoughts even when I hold you in my arms.' He stretched them towards her. 'Lucy, I have cared for you since that man died in the square. I cannot live without you.'

'And Mr Vyse,' said Lucy, who kept admirably calm. 'Does it not matter that I love Cecil and shall be his wife soon?'

He said, 'It is our last chance.' He turned to Miss Bartlett. 'You wouldn't stop us this second time if you understood.'

Miss Bartlett did not answer.

'I am certain that Lucy cares for me really,' he said quietly. He left them, carefully closing the front door. They watched him walk away from the house.

'Oh, Lucy – oh, what an awful man!'

Lucy did not react. 'Well, he amuses me,' she said. 'Either I'm mad, or he is, and I think he is. Anyway, I don't think my admirer will trouble me again.'

They went outside. Lucy was filled with some strong emotion – pity, terror, love – and she was aware of autumn. Summer was ending.

'Hello, Lucy! It's still light enough to play one more game of tennis,' Freddy called out to her.

'Mr Emerson has had to leave.'

'What a nuisance! Cecil, do play, do. Just this once.'

Cecil's voice came. 'My dear Freddy, I am not athletic. As you remarked so accurately this morning, "There are some people who are only suited to studying books". I am guilty of being one of those people, and will not force myself on you.'

Lucy saw the truth. How had she tolerated Cecil for one moment? He was absolutely awful. The same evening she ended their engagement.

◆

Cecil was confused. He had nothing to say. He was not even angry, but stood with a glass of whisky between his hands, trying to think what had led her to such a conclusion.

Lucy had chosen the moment before bed to talk to Cecil. They were alone in the sitting room.

'I am very sorry about it,' she said. 'I have thought about it carefully. We are too different.'

'Different – how – how – ?'

'I haven't had a good education,' she continued. 'My Italian trip came too late, and I am forgetting all that I learned there. I shall never be able to talk to your friends, or behave as a wife of yours should.'

'I don't understand. You aren't behaving normally. You're tired, Lucy.'

'Tired!' she cried. 'That is exactly like you. You always think women don't mean what they say. I can't marry you, and you will thank me for saying so one day.'

'Give me a moment.' Cecil closed his eyes. 'You must excuse me if I say stupid things, but my brain has gone to pieces. Three minutes ago, I was sure that you loved me. Now – I find it difficult – I am likely to say the wrong thing.'

She realised that he was behaving rather well, and she became more annoyed. She again desired a struggle, not a discussion. To bring the crisis closer, she said, 'There are days when one sees things clearly, and this is one of them. If you want to know, it was quite a little thing that made me decide to speak to you – when you wouldn't play tennis with Freddy.'

'But I never play tennis,' said Cecil, very confused. 'I never could play. I don't understand a word. Why couldn't you have warned me if you felt there was something wrong? You talked about our wedding at lunch – at least, you let me talk.'

'I knew you wouldn't understand,' said Lucy, quite crossly. 'Of course, it isn't just the tennis. I have been feeling like this for weeks, but surely it was better not to speak till I felt certain. I have often wondered if I was suitable to be your wife – for instance, in London; and are you suitable to be my husband? I don't think so. You don't like Freddy, or my mother. There were always things wrong with our engagement, Cecil, but our relations seemed pleased, and we met so often, and it was no good mentioning it until – well, until I had to. Today I see clearly. I must speak. That's all.'

'I cannot think you were right,' said Cecil gently. 'I cannot tell why, but though all you say sounds true, I feel that you are not treating me fairly. It's all too horrible. But surely I have a right to hear a little more?'

'I really think we ought to go to bed,' Lucy said. 'I shall only say things that will make me unhappy afterwards.'

But Cecil now found her more desirable each moment. He looked at her, instead of through her, for the first time since they were engaged. In a burst of genuine emotion, he cried, 'But I love you, and I did think you loved me!'

'I did not,' she said. 'I thought I did at first. I am sorry, and I ought to have refused you this last time too.'

He began to walk up and down the room. He was behaving so well. It would have been easier for her if he had behaved badly.

'You don't love me, that is clear. You are probably right not to. But it would hurt a little less if I knew why.'

George's phrase came into her mind. 'Because you're the sort of person who can't have a close relationship with anyone. I don't mean exactly that. But you insist on questioning me, even though I beg you not to. Before, you let me behave as I wanted. Now, you're always protecting me. Can't I be trusted? You despise my mother because she is conventional, and worries about puddings; but – ' She rose to her feet. 'Cecil, you're conventional, because though you may understand beautiful things, you don't know how to use them. You wrap yourself up in art and books and music, and try to wrap me up, too. I won't be silenced, not by the most wonderful music. People are more wonderful, and you hide them from me. That's why I am breaking off my engagement. You were all right as long as you concentrated on things, but when you spent time with people – ' She stopped.

There was a pause. Then Cecil said with great emotion, 'It is true. You are even greater than I thought. You are much too good to me. I shall never forget your understanding. Dear, I only blame you for *this*: you could have warned me earlier, and so given me a chance to improve. I have never known you till this evening. This evening you are a different person: new thoughts − even a new voice − '

Then she lost her control. 'If you think I am in love with someone else, you are very much mistaken.'

'Of course I don't think that. You are not that kind, Lucy.' His voice broke. 'I must thank you for what you have done − for showing me what I really am. Will you shake hands?'

'Of course I will,' said Lucy. 'Good night, Cecil. Goodbye. I'm sorry about it. Thank you very much for your gentleness.'

They went into the hall.

'Thank you, Lucy. Good night again.'

'Goodbye, Cecil.'

She watched him go upstairs. Halfway up he paused, and gave her a look of memorable beauty.

She could never marry. Cecil believed in her; she must one day believe in herself. She must become one of those women whom she had praised, who care for freedom and not for men. She must forget that George loved her, that George had gone away. She must not think, or feel. She was no longer true to herself. She pretended to George that she did not love him, and pretended to Cecil that she loved no one. It had been the same for Miss Bartlett thirty years before.

Chapter 13   Lucy Decides to Go to Greece

On Monday afternoon, Mr Beebe bicycled over to Windy Corner with a little piece of gossip. He had heard from the Miss Alans. These admirable ladies, since they could not go to Cissie Villa, had changed their plans. They were going to Greece instead. In the letter, Miss Catharine Alan asked Mr Beebe if he

81

knew of an English church in Athens. It was possible they might go as far as Constantinople.⋆ Did Mr Beebe know a really comfortable pension there?

Mr Beebe thought that this letter would amuse Lucy. So, knowing nothing about what had happened the day before, he was cycling over to Windy Corner to get some tea, to see his niece, and to show Lucy the letter.

At the top of the hill, Mr Beebe saw a carriage in the entrance to Windy Corner. The horse was not able to pull the carriage full of people up the hill, so passengers were expected to walk for that part of the journey. Mr Beebe stood and watched as Cecil and Freddy got out of the carriage. There was a suitcase by the driver. Cecil wore a hat, so he must be going away, while Freddy was accompanying him to the station. They came up the hill towards Mr Beebe, overtaking the carriage. They shook hands with the clergyman, but did not speak.

'So you're leaving us for a while, Mr Vyse?' Mr Beebe asked.

Cecil said, 'Yes,' while Freddy moved away.

'I was coming to show you this delightful letter from those friends of Miss Honeychurch.' He quoted from it. 'Isn't it wonderful? Isn't it romantic?'

Cecil listened politely, and said he was sure that Lucy would be amused and interested.

'Mr Beebe,' said Freddy, 'have you any matches?'

'*I* have,' said Cecil, and Mr Beebe noticed that he spoke to the boy more kindly.

'You have never met these Miss Alans, have you, Mr Vyse?' asked Mr Beebe.

'Never.'

'Then you don't see the wonder of this Greek visit. I haven't been to Greece, and don't intend to go, and I can't imagine any

⋆Constantinople: now the Turkish city of Istanbul

82

of my friends going. It's too big an adventure for people like us. Don't you think so? Italy is as much as we can manage. Freddy, give me those matches when you've finished with them.' He lit a cigarette, and went on talking to the two young men. 'I was saying, we are more suited to Italy. That's enough for us to understand. Ah! The carriage has arrived.'

'You're quite right,' said Cecil, and got into the carriage. Freddy followed, nodding to the clergyman.

They had only gone a short distance when the carriage stopped again. Freddy jumped out, and came running back for Cecil's matchbox, which had not been returned. As he took it, Freddy said to Mr Beebe, 'Cecil's very upset. Lucy won't marry him.'

'But when?'

'Late last night. I must go.'

'Perhaps I shouldn't visit your family.'

'No – go on. Goodbye.'

'Oh, good!' said Mr Beebe to himself. 'Her engagement to Cecil was the one stupid thing that Lucy did.'

When he arrived at Windy Corner, Lucy was playing the piano in the sitting room. He hesitated for a moment, and then went into the garden. There he found a sad group. It was a windy day, and some of the flowers were damaged. Mrs Honeychurch, who looked cross, was tying them up, while Miss Bartlett, dressed in unsuitable clothes for gardening, interrupted her with offers of assistance. Minnie was standing near them, holding some string.

'Oh, how do you do, Mr Beebe? What a mess everything is! Look at my flowers!'

Mrs Honeychurch was visibly upset. Minnie ran up to her uncle and whispered that everyone was very bad-tempered.

'Come for a walk with me,' he told her. 'Mrs Honeychurch, may I take her out to tea at the Beehive Inn?'

'Yes, do. No, I don't need the scissors, thank you, Charlotte – my hands are full.'

Mr Beebe invited Charlotte to join them. Mrs Honeychurch encouraged her to go. Miss Bartlett said that her duty was to stay at Windy Corner. After annoying everyone except Minnie by refusing to accept the invitation, she turned round and annoyed Minnie by accepting it.

They walked up the garden.

'Perhaps Miss Honeychurch would like to come with us?' suggested Mr Beebe.

'I think we'd better leave Lucy alone,' Charlotte answered. Minnie went upstairs to put her boots on. Mr Beebe went into the sitting room. Lucy was still playing the piano. She stopped when he entered.

'How do you do? Miss Bartlett and Minnie are coming with me to tea at the Beehive Inn. Will you come too?'

'I don't think I will, thank you.' Lucy played a few notes on the piano.

'Miss Honeychurch!'

'Yes.'

'I met them on the hill. Your brother told me.'

'Oh, did he?' She sounded annoyed.

'I assure you that the news will go no further.'

'Mother, Charlotte, Cecil, Freddy, you,' said Lucy, playing a note for each person who knew, and then playing a sixth note.

'If you'll let me say so, I am very glad, and I am certain that you have done the right thing.'

'I hoped other people would think so, but they don't seem to.'

'I could see that Miss Bartlett thought your decision was unwise.'

'So does Mother,' replied Lucy. 'Mother is very upset.'

Mrs Honeychurch, who hated all changes, did mind, but not nearly as much as Lucy pretended.

Mr Beebe saw that Lucy — very properly — did not want to discuss her action, so he said, 'I have had a ridiculous letter from

Miss Catharine Alan. That was why I came to visit you. I thought it might amuse you.'

'How delightful!' said Lucy, in a dull voice.

In order to have something to do, he began to read her the letter. After a few words, her eyes looked brighter, and soon she interrupted him with – 'Going abroad? When?'

'Next week, they say.'

'How perfectly splendid of the Miss Alans to go abroad! I wish I could go with them,' exclaimed Lucy. 'I have always wanted to go to Constantinople. It's almost in Asia, isn't it?'

Mr Beebe reminded her that Constantinople was unlikely, and that the Miss Alans were just aiming to go to Athens, and maybe one other place in Greece. But Lucy was still enthusiastic. She wanted to go to Greece even more, it seemed. He was surprised to see that she was serious.

'I didn't realise that you and the Miss Alans were such friends, after Cissie Villa,' he said.

'Oh, that's nothing. I really want to go with them.'

'Would your mother allow it? You have been home less than three months?'

'She *must* allow it!' cried Lucy, becoming more excited. 'I *must* go away. I have to go away.'

Mr Beebe did not really understand her. Why could she not stay with her family?

'I'm afraid it has been a difficult business for you,' he said gently.

'No, not at all. Cecil was very kind indeed; but – I had better tell you the whole truth, since you have heard a little. It was because he wouldn't let me do what I wanted. He wanted to improve me. Cecil won't let a woman decide for herself. Oh, what nonsense I am talking!'

'It is what I understood from observing Mr Vyse. I am very sympathetic, and I completely agree with you. But is it worth rushing off to Greece?'

'But I must go somewhere!' Lucy cried.

At that moment Miss Bartlett entered the room.

'Come along; tea, tea, tea,' said Mr Beebe, and hurried out of the front door with the others.

On the way to tea, he prepared himself to discuss Lucy with Miss Bartlett.

'It is very important,' said Miss Bartlett, 'that there should be no gossip in Summer Street. It would be *death* to gossip about Mr Vyse's dismissal at the present moment.'

Mr Beebe raised his eyebrows. 'Of course, Miss Honeychurch will tell people in her own way, and when she chooses. Freddy only told me because he knew she would not mind.'

'I know,' replied Miss Bartlett. 'But Freddy ought not to have told even you. We have to be very careful.'

They walked up the hill in silence. From time to time, the vicar would name some flower. At the top of the hill they paused.

'It isn't going to rain, but it will be dark soon. Let us hurry on,' said Mr Beebe.

They reached the Beehive Inn at about five o'clock. Mr Beebe and Miss Bartlett sat inside; Minnie stayed outside, and was given food through the window.

'I have been thinking, Miss Bartlett,' said Mr Beebe. 'I don't know if you heard us talking about it, but Lucy wants to join the Miss Alans in their extraordinary travel plans.' He pulled the letter from the Miss Alans out of his pocket. 'I can't explain — it's wrong.'

Miss Bartlett read the letter in silence. He was astonished when she replied, 'I think it would save Lucy.'

'Really. Why?'

'She wanted to leave Windy Corner,' said Miss Bartlett. 'It is natural, surely — after such painful scenes — that she should desire a change.'

'But why need she go as far as Greece?' asked Mr Beebe.

'That is a good question,' replied Miss Bartlett. 'Why Greece? Why not Tunbridge Wells? Oh, Mr Beebe! I had a long and most unsatisfactory interview with dear Lucy this morning. I cannot help her. I will say no more. Perhaps I have already said too much. I wanted her to spend six months with me at Tunbridge Wells, and she refused.'

Mr Beebe said, 'I want your advice.'

'Very well,' said Charlotte. 'I will help her go to Greece. Will you? She must not stay here any longer, and we must keep quiet until she goes. But Lucy and I cannot persuade Mrs Honeychurch alone. If you help, we may succeed.'

'Yes, I will help her,' said the clergyman. 'Come, let us return now, and settle everything.'

Miss Bartlett was full of gratitude. Mr Beebe did not quite understand the situation, but he did not desire to understand it. He had never believed in marriage, and whenever he heard that an engagement had been broken off, he had a slight feeling of pleasure.

They hurried home. In the garden Mrs Honeychurch, now helped by Freddy, was still tying up her flowers.

'It's too dark,' Mrs Honeychurch said, 'and now Lucy wants to go to Greece. I don't know what's happening to the world.'

'Mrs Honeychurch,' Mr Beebe said, 'Lucy must go to Greece. Come into the house, and we'll talk about it. Do you mind about her ending her engagement to Mr Vyse?'

'Mr Beebe, I'm thankful – simply thankful.'

'So am I,' said Freddy.

'Good. Now come up to the house.'

They talked in the dining room for half an hour. The Greek idea was expensive and dramatic – both qualities that Lucy's mother hated. But Mr Beebe managed to influence Mrs Honeychurch.

'I don't see why Greece is necessary,' she said. 'However, as you do, I suppose it is all right. Lucy! Let's tell her. Lucy!'

Mrs Honeychurch went into the sitting room, and Mr Beebe heard her kiss Lucy and say, 'I am sorry I was so cross about Greece, but I was upset about the flowers. And you are right, too – Greece will be all right. You can go if the Miss Alans will take you.'

'Oh, splendid! Oh, thank you!'

Mr Beebe went into the room. Lucy sat at the piano. Her mother bent over her. Freddy lay on the floor with his head against her, and an unlit pipe between his lips. It was a beautiful scene. Mr Beebe looked at them. Why should Lucy want either to marry or to travel when she had such friends at home?

Chapter 14   Lucy Discovers Her True Feelings

The Miss Alans were staying in a hotel in London. They always stayed there before travelling, and for a week or two would think about clothes, guidebooks, food supplies and other necessary items. It did not occur to them that there are shops abroad; they saw travel as a type of battle, for which you needed to have the right equipment. They hoped Miss Honeychurch would bring the right things. Lucy promised, feeling a little depressed.

'But of course, you know all about travelling, and you have Mr Vyse to help you.'

Mrs Honeychurch, who had come to London with her daughter, began to drum her fingers nervously on the table.

'We think it is so good of Mr Vyse to let you come with us,' said Miss Catharine. 'It is not every man who would be so unselfish. But perhaps he will come out and join you later. However, we shall see him when he comes to say goodbye. I do want to meet him.'

'No one will be coming to see Lucy leave,' interrupted Mrs Honeychurch. 'She doesn't like it.'

'Really, how funny! I should have thought that in this situation – Oh, Mrs Honeychurch, you aren't going? It is such a pleasure to have met you.'

They escaped, and Lucy said with relief, 'That's all right. We coped this time.'

But her mother was annoyed. 'I cannot see why you didn't tell your friends about Cecil. We had to sit there almost telling lies, which they may have realised. It was most unpleasant.'

Lucy described the Miss Alans' character. They were terrible gossips, and if one told them, the news would be everywhere in no time.

'But why shouldn't the news be everywhere in no time?' asked Mrs Honeychurch.

'Because I agreed with Cecil not to announce it until I left England. I shall tell them then. How wet it is! Let's go to a bookshop so I can buy a guidebook.'

'You know, Lucy,' said Mrs Honeychurch, 'you and Charlotte and Mr Beebe all tell me I'm so stupid, so I suppose I am, but I shall never understand all this. You got rid of Cecil and I'm thankful he's gone, though I did feel angry for a minute. But why not announce it?'

Lucy was silent. She was becoming less close to her mother. It would have been quite easy to say, 'Because George Emerson has been bothering me, and if he hears I have given up Cecil, he may begin again.' It was true. But she did not like describing her inner thoughts. Ever since that last evening in Florence, she thought that it was an unwise thing to reveal her soul.

Mrs Honeychurch, too, was silent. Then she burst out, 'You're tired of Windy Corner.'

That was perfectly true. Lucy no longer felt that she belonged at Windy Corner. She was annoyed, and upset. 'Oh, Mother, what rubbish you talk!' They entered the bookshop. 'Of course I want to live at home, but I shall want to be away in the future more than I have been before. You see, I will have my own money next year.'

Her mother's eyes filled with tears.

Lucy continued, 'I've seen so little of the world. I ought to come up to London more. I might even share a flat with some other girl.'

Lucy's mother exploded. 'And try and get a secretarial job. And call it Work, when thousands of men are without jobs. And prepare yourself for this by going abroad with two old ladies.'

'I want more independence,' said Lucy, weakly.

'Very well,' said her mother. 'Take your independence and go. Leave the house that your father built, and the garden he planted, and our dear view – and share a flat with another girl.'

Lucy made a face, and said, 'Perhaps I spoke hastily.'

'You do remind me of Charlotte Bartlett!' her mother said.

'*Charlotte?*' repeated Lucy angrily, upset by this comment. 'I don't know what you mean, Mother. Charlotte and I are not at all alike.'

'Well, I see the similarity. The same endless worrying, the same withdrawing of what you say. You and Charlotte trying to divide two apples among three people last night might have been sisters.'

Lucy and her mother shopped in silence, spoke little in the train, and little in the carriage which met them at the station. It had rained all day, and it was hot inside the carriage. They were going to collect Charlotte at Summer Street, where she had gone to visit Mr Beebe's mother.

'Can we have some air in the carriage?' Lucy demanded.

Her mother, with sudden tenderness, said, 'Very well.' The horse was stopped, and Lucy saw that there were no lights in the windows of Cissie Villa, and it looked as if the gate was locked.

'Is that house empty again?' she asked the driver.

'Yes, miss,' he replied. 'It is too far away from town for the young gentleman, and his father is not able to walk very far, so he can't stay there alone. They've gone.'

The carriage stopped at the vicarage. Lucy got out to call for Miss Bartlett. So the Emersons had gone, and all this bother about Greece had been unnecessary. Waste! That was what her life was about. Wasted plans, wasted money, wasted love, and she had wounded her mother. When the maid opened the door, she was unable to speak, and stared stupidly into the hall.

Miss Bartlett came forward. She would like to go to church, if that was all right with her hostess.

'Certainly,' said Mrs Honeychurch, sounding tired. 'Let's all go. The carriage can wait here for us.'

'No church for me, thank you,' said Lucy. The maid suggested that she waited in Mr Beebe's study.

Old Mr Emerson was sitting by the fire. 'Oh, Miss Honeychurch, you have come,' he said in a faint voice. Lucy saw that he had altered since she had last seen him.

She said nothing. She could have coped with George, but she had forgotten how to treat his father.

'Miss Honeychurch, dear, we are so sorry! George is so sorry! I cannot blame my boy, but I wish he had told me first. He ought not to have tried. I knew nothing about it at all.'

If only she could remember how to behave! She turned her back, and began to look at Mr Beebe's books.

'I taught him,' said Mr Emerson, his voice shaking, 'to trust in love. I said, "the woman you love, she is the only person you will ever really understand."' He sighed. 'Poor boy! He is so sorry! But,' – his voice became stronger – 'Miss Honeychurch, do you remember Italy?'

Lucy selected a book. Holding it up to her eyes, she said, 'I have no wish to discuss Italy or any subject connected with your son. His behaviour was terrible. I am glad he is sorry. Do you know what he did?'

91

'It wasn't terrible,' Mr Emerson gently corrected her. 'He only tried when he should not have tried. You have all you want, Miss Honeychurch; you are going to marry the man you love. Do not go out of George's life saying he is terrible.'

'No, of course,' said Lucy, ashamed at the mention of Cecil. 'I think I will go to church after all. I shall not be very late – '

'George has gone under. Like his mother did.'

'But, Mr Emerson – *Mr Emerson* – what are you talking about?'

'When I wouldn't have George baptized,' he said.

Lucy was frightened.

'She agreed that baptism was unimportant, but he got ill when he was twelve, and she thought it was a punishment. Mr Eager – he came while I was out, and acted according to his principles. I don't blame him or anyone – but by the time George was well, she was ill. Mr Eager made her think about sin, and she died thinking about it.'

So that was how Mr Emerson had murdered his wife in the sight of God.

'Oh, how terrible!' said Lucy, finally forgetting her own affairs. She asked if young Mr Emerson was ill.

'George is not ill. He is never ill. But he will not think it worthwhile to live. He will live, but he will never think that anything is worthwhile.'

'I am so sorry, but it is no good discussing this affair. I am really deeply sorry about it,' said Lucy.

'Ah well, George comes down tomorrow to collect me, and I will stay with him in London. He cannot bear to be here, and I must be where he is.'

'Mr Emerson,' cried the girl, 'don't leave – at least, not because of me. I am going to Greece. Don't leave your comfortable house.'

It was the first time her voice had been kind, and he smiled.

'How good everyone is! And look at Mr Beebe, inviting me to stay! But I must be with George. He says the thought of seeing you and hearing about you – I am not excusing him; I am only saying what happened.'

'Oh, Mr Emerson,' – she took hold of his hand – 'you mustn't. I don't want you moving out of your house when you like it, and perhaps losing money through it – all because of me. You must stay. I am going to Greece.'

'To Greece?'

'So you must stay. We won't talk about this business. I know I can trust you both.'

'Certainly you can. I suppose Mr Vyse is very angry with George? No, it was wrong of George to try.'

She looked at the books again. He was certain she was tired, and offered her his chair.

'No, please sit still. I think I will sit in the carriage.' Her lips were trembling.

'Greece – but you were going to be married this year, I thought.'

'Not till January,' said Lucy. Would she tell a lie?

'I hope that you will enjoy Greece with Mr Vyse.'

'Thank you.'

At that moment, Mr Beebe came back from church. 'It's raining again. Your cousin and mother are waiting at the church for the carriage to collect them.' He hurried out to the stables.

'He is not going,' said Lucy. 'I made a mistake. Mr Vyse is staying in England.' It was impossible to lie to this old man.

'You are leaving the man you love?'

'I – I had to.'

'Why, Miss Honeychurch, why?'

She was overcome with terror, and she lied again. She made the long speech she had made to Mr Beebe. He heard her in silence and then said, 'My dear, I am worried about you. It seems to me that you are in a muddle.'

She shook her head.

'Listen to an old man. There's nothing worse than a muddle in the whole world. It's easy to face death and fate, and the things that sound so awful. It is my muddles I regret. All my teaching of George has come to this: avoid muddle. Do you remember in the church, when you pretended to be annoyed with me, and weren't? Do you remember before when you refused the room with the view? Those were muddles – little, but threatening – and I fear you are in a muddle now.' She was silent. 'Do trust me, Miss Honeychurch. Though life is very wonderful, it is difficult.' Then he burst out excitedly, 'You love George!' The three words burst against Lucy like waves on the open sea.

'How dare you!' cried Lucy. 'You suppose that a woman is always thinking about a man.'

'But you are. You're shocked, but I intend to shock you. I can reach you in no other way. You must marry, or your life will be wasted. I know that you love George. Then be his wife. It isn't possible to love and to part. You can change love, ignore it, muddle it, but you can never pull it out of you. The poets are right. Love lasts for ever.'

Lucy began to cry with anger, and though her anger soon disappeared, her tears remained.

'What nonsense I have talked. And I have made you cry. Dear girl, forgive me, marry my boy.'

She could not understand him, but as he spoke, the darkness was withdrawn, and she saw to the bottom of her soul.

'You've frightened me,' she cried. 'Cecil – Mr Beebe – the tickets bought – everything.' She fell crying into the chair. 'I'm caught in the muddle.' A carriage arrived at the front door. 'Give George my love – once only. Tell him, "Muddle".' Then she arranged her hat, while the tears poured down her cheeks. 'They are in the hall – oh, please not, Mr Emerson – they trust me – '

'But why should they, when you have deceived them?'

Mr Beebe opened the door. 'What's that?' he said sharply.

'I was saying, why should you trust her when she has deceived you?'

Mr Beebe came in and shut the door.

'I don't understand you, Mr Emerson. To whom do you refer?'

'I mean, she has pretended to you that she did not love George. They have loved each other from the beginning.'

Mr Beebe looked at the crying girl. He was very quiet.

'Mr Beebe – I have deceived you – I have deceived myself.'

'Oh, rubbish, Miss Honeychurch!'

'Lucy! Lucy!' called voices from the carriage.

'Mr Beebe, could you help me?'

He looked amazed at the request, and said in a low, serious voice, 'I am more upset than I can possible say. It is awful, awful. I can't believe it.'

'What's wrong with the boy?' demanded Mr Emerson.

'Nothing, Mr Emerson, except that he no longer interests me. Marry George, Miss Honeychurch. He is an admirable choice.'

He walked out and left them.

Lucy, desperate, turned to Mr Emerson. His face gave her courage. It was the face of a saint who understood.

'Now it is all dark. But remember the mountains over Florence and the view. Ah, dear, if I were George, and gave you one kiss, it would make you brave. You have to go cold into a battle, out into the muddle that you have made yourself. Your mother and all your friends will despise you.' Into his own eyes tears came. 'We fight for more than Love or Pleasure; there is Truth. Truth matters.'

'You kiss me,' said the girl. 'I will try.'

He gave her the feeling that, in gaining the man she loved, she would gain something for the whole world. He had shown her the holiness of direct desire. She never exactly understood, she would say in later years, how he managed to strengthen her. It was as if he had made her see the whole of everything at once.

Chapter 15   Return to the Pension Bertolini

The Miss Alans did go to Greece, but they went by themselves. We return to the Pension Bertolini.

George said it was his old room.

'No, it isn't,' said Lucy, 'because it is the room I had, and I had your father's room. I forget why; Charlotte made me, for some reason.'

He knelt on the floor, and laid his head in her lap.

'George, you baby, get up.'

'Why shouldn't I be a baby?'

Unable to answer this question, she put down his sock, which she was trying to mend, and stared out through the window. It was evening, and spring again.

'Oh, bother Charlotte,' she said thoughtfully. 'What can such people be made of?'

'The same stuff as vicars are made of.'

'Nonsense! Now get up off the cold floor, or you'll be stiff tomorrow, and stop laughing and being so silly.'

'Why shouldn't I laugh?' he asked her, his face close to hers. 'What's there to cry at? Kiss me here.' He indicated the spot where a kiss would be welcome.

He was just a boy. She found it charming, in a strange way, that he was sometimes wrong.

'Any letters?' he asked.

'Just one from Freddy.'

'Now kiss me here; then here.'

He walked to the window and leant out. He felt gratitude for the people who had taken so much trouble for a young fool. All the fighting that mattered had been done by others – by Italy, by his father, by his wife. And the people who had not meant to help – the Miss Lavishes, the Cecils, the Miss Bartletts! George counted up all the forces that had contributed to his contentment.

'Anything good in Freddy's letter?'

'Not yet.'

His content was complete, hers still held bitterness. The Honeychurches had not forgiven them; they were disgusted by her pretence. She was separated from Windy Corner, perhaps for ever.

'What does he say?'

'Silly boy. He knew we would go off in the spring – he has known for six months that if Mother would not agree to our marriage, we would have to leave, and get married. They had enough warning. But it will all come right in the end. I wish, though, that Cecil had not become so pessimistic about women. He has, for the second time, quite altered. I wish, too, that Mr Beebe he will never forgive us – I mean, he will never be interested in us again. I wish that he did not influence them so much at Windy Corner. I wish he hadn't – but if we act the truth, the people who really love us are sure to come back to us in the end.'

'Perhaps.' Then he said, more gently, 'Well, I acted the truth – the only thing I did do – and you came back to me. So possibly you know.' He turned back into the room, picked her up and carried her to the window so that she, too, saw all the view. They knelt down, hoping they were invisible from the road, and began to whisper one another's names. Ah! It was worthwhile; it was the great joy that they had expected, and numerous little joys of which they had never dreamt. They were silent. Outside the window, they heard the voice of a cab driver, '*Signorino, domani faremo un giro.*'*

---

*Signorino, domani faremo un giro: the Italian for 'Sir, tomorrow let's go for a drive.'

'Oh, bother that man!'

But Lucy said, 'No, don't be rude to him.' Then she murmured, 'Mr Eager and Charlotte, awful frozen Charlotte! How cruel she would be to a man like that! This room reminds me of Charlotte. How horrible to grow old like Charlotte. And think about that evening at the vicarage. If she had known your father was in the house, she would have stopped me from going into the study, and he was the only person alive who could have made me understand what I really wanted. You couldn't have made me. When I am very happy,' – she kissed him – 'I only remember what a tiny thing was responsible. If Charlotte had known, she would have stopped me going into the study, and I would have gone to silly Greece, and become different for ever.'

'But she did know,' said George. 'She saw my father. He said so.'

'Oh, no, she didn't see him. She was upstairs with Mr Beebe's mother, don't you remember, and then went straight to the church. She said so.'

George was firm. 'My father saw her, and I prefer his word. He was half asleep by the study fire, and he opened his eyes, and there was Miss Bartlett. A few minutes before you came in. She was turning to go as he woke up. He didn't speak to her.'

Then they spoke of other things. It was a long time before they returned to Miss Bartlett, but when they did, her behaviour seemed more interesting. George, who disliked any darkness, said, 'It's clear that she knew. Then, why did she risk the meeting? She knew he was there, but she went to church.'

They tried to put all the pieces together. As they talked, an extraordinary solution came into Lucy's mind. She rejected it, and said, 'How like Charlotte to undo her work by a stupid muddle at the last moment.' But something in the dying evening, in the roar of the river, in their embrace, warned her that her words were not quite right, and George whispered, 'Or did she mean to?'

'Mean what?'

'*Signorino, domani faremo un giro.*'

Lucy bent forward and said with gentleness, '*Lascia, prego, lascia. Siamo sposati.*'★

'*Scusi tanto, signora,*'★ he replied, in as gentle a voice.

George whispered, 'Is this possible? I'll tell you something wonderful. Your cousin has always hoped. From the very first moment that we met, she hoped, deep down in her mind, that we would be like this. She fought us on the surface, but she still hoped. I can't explain her any other way. Can you? She is not frozen, Lucy. She separated us twice, but in the vicarage that evening she was given one more chance to make us happy. We can never make friends with her or thank her. But I do believe that deep in her heart, far below all speech and behaviour, she is glad.'

'It is impossible,' murmured Lucy, and then, remembering the experiences of her own heart, she said, 'No — it is just possible.'

They were lost in their own youth. There was shared passion; they had found love. But they were conscious of a love that was even more mysterious than theirs. Outside they could hear the river, bringing the snows of winter down towards the sea.

★*Lascia, prego, lascia. Siamo sposati*: the Italian for 'Leave it, please. We are married.'

★*Scusi tanto, signora*: the Italian for 'So sorry, madam.'

ACTIVITIES

Chapters 1–3

Before you read

1 Discuss these questions with another student. What do you think?

    a Which of the following qualities would your parents consider most important in your future partner? Why? Number them in order of importance.

    a loving and kind personality   a smart appearance
the same social class   the same religion   a similar age
a good career   good table manners

    b Which of the qualities above would have been important to parents a hundred years ago, do you think? Why?

    c In your country, how has the influence of family and society on the choice of marriage partner changed over the last century?

    d Describe the best view from a room that you have ever had. What made the view so special for you?

2 Look at the Word List at the back of the book. Find words for

    a people and activities connected with religion.

    b other people.

    c actions that express feelings.

    d forms of transport.

While you read

3 Write in the missing names.

    a .... is angry about her rooms and .... wishes the pension felt more Italian.

    b .... offers to exchange rooms with .... and ....

    c .... wants .... to change her mind about leaving the pension when she sees ....

    d .... and .... go to the church of Santa Croce while .... stays in the pension.

e In the church of Santa Croce, ... is annoyed by
........................'s interruptions.

f .... asks .... to be friendly with
....

g .... becomes good friends with .... ,
who is writing a novel about modern Italy.

h .... and .... disapprove of
.... going out alone.

i .... helps .... after she sees a murder.

After you read

4 Find the correct endings, below, to these sentences.

   a The guests dislike Mr Emerson because he ...   .

   b Lucy is pleased to see Mr Beebe because he ...   .

   c Lucy bows to Mr Emerson and his son because she ...   .

   d Miss Bartlett refuses Mr Emerson's offer because
she ...   .

   e Lucy and Mr Beebe are secretly delighted because
Miss Bartlett ...   .

   f Lucy feels confused in the church of Santa Croce
because she ...   .

   g George is unhappy because the world ...   .

   h Miss Alan thinks that Miss Lavish is strange because
she ...   .

   i Lucy feels ashamed because she ...   .

   j Lucy's heart warms towards George because he ...   .

   1) talks to the Emersons in the smoking room.

   2) is the new local vicar.

   3) is embarrassed by George.

   4) enjoys the company of people she should not be with.

   5) faints in public.

   6) does not want to appear unkind.

   7) seems confused about the photographs.

   8) makes no sense.

   9) feels superior and distrusts his motives.

   10) comes from a different social background.

5 How do these people feel about the Emersons? Why?

    a Miss Bartlett

    b Lucy

    c Mr Beebe

    d Miss Lavish

    e Miss Alan

    f the other guests

6 Discuss these questions.

    a What does Miss Bartlett find in her new room? What does it suggest about the room's previous occupant?

    b How do Lucy and George feel after the incident in the Piazza Signoria? Why?

    c What have you learnt in this part of the book about English tourists at that time?

Chapters 4–6

Before you read

7 How do you think the other English people will react to Lucy's adventure?

While you read

8 Mark each statement T (true) or F (false).

    a Miss Bartlett is angry with Lucy after the incident in the Piazza Signoria. .....

    b Lucy visits the Torre del Gallo. .....

    c Lucy does not want to be a character in Miss Lavish's novel. .....

    d Mr Eager believes that Mr Emerson murdered his wife. .....

    e Lucy shares a carriage with Mr Eager, Mr Emerson and George. .....

    f Miss Bartlett sees George kissing Lucy. .....

    g Freddy is happy about his sister's engagement to Cecil. .....

    h Lucy first met Cecil in Rome. .....

i	Cecil does not need to work.	.....
j	Mr Beebe learns of Lucy's engagement from her mother.	.....

After you read

9 How do these people feel, and why?

    a Lucy, when Miss Bartlett stops to look at the river.

    b Lucy, about events in the Piazza Signoria.

    c Miss Lavish, about events in the Piazza Signoria.

    d Lucy, about Mr Eager and Miss Lavish.

    e Mr Eager, about Mr Emerson and Miss Lavish.

    f Mr Emerson, about the Italian driver's behaviour.

    g Lucy, after George kisses her.

    h Lucy's mother and brother, about Cecil.

    i Cecil, about Lucy after Italy.

    j Mr Beebe, about Lucy's musical ability.

10 Work with another student. Have this conversation.

    Student A: You are Mr Emerson. You think that George would be a better husband for Lucy. Explain why.

    Student B: You are Mrs Honeychurch. You think that Cecil would be a better husband for Lucy. Say why.

Chapters 7–9

Before you read

11 Do you think Lucy will be happy with Cecil? Why (not)?

While you read

12 Circle the correct word or phrase.

    a Cecil is *impressed/unimpressed* by the people in Lucy's neighbourhood.

    b Sir Harry Otway is *ashamed/proud* of the two villas he bought.

    c Cecil thinks that Lucy is too *adventurous/unadventurous*.

    d *Lucy/Mr Beebe* tells Mrs Honeychurch about the Emersons in Florence.

    e Cecil offers the Emersons the empty villa because *they are friends of his/he wants to embarrass Sir Harry*.

f Lucy *approves / disapproves* of Cecil's arrangements for the villa.

g Lucy is *annoyed / pleased* by Miss Bartlett's letter.

h *Mr Beebe / George* thinks that the Emersons' arrival in the area is due to fate.

i George is *shy / cheerful* when he meets Lucy and her mother by the pool.

After you read

13 Who is speaking and to whom? What is the speaker talking about?

    a 'Their attitude is wrong.'

    b 'I fear it will attract the wrong type of people.'

    c 'Everyone – even your mother – is deceived by him.'

    d 'You could have asked before.'

    e 'There *is* a right sort and a wrong sort and it's silly to pretend there isn't.'

    f 'Poor little ladies! So shocked and so pleased!'

    g 'I consider it most disloyal of you.'

    h 'Italy has done it.'

    i 'These two young people are going to be friends.'

    j 'Whoever were these unfortunate people?'

14 Discuss how Lucy and Cecil react to these situations. Who do you feel most sympathetic towards? Why?

    a the garden party

    b Sir Harry's problem with Cissie Villa

    c the walk home from Cissie Villa

    d Italy

    e the arrival of Mr Emerson and George at Cissie Villa

    f the nude bathers

Chapters 10–12

Before you read

15 How do you think the arrival of George at Cissie Villa will affect Lucy in the next part of the story?

While you read

16 Put these events in the right order, 1–10

    a George criticises Cecil.   .....

    b Mrs Honeychurch is formally introduced to
Mr Emerson.   .....

    c Cecil reads aloud from Miss Lavish's novel.   .....

    d Mrs Honeychurch criticises Cecil.   .....

    e Lucy ends her engagement.   .....

    f Miss Bartlett arrives at Windy Corner.   .....

    g George kisses Lucy.   .....

    h Miss Bartlett and Lucy discuss events in Italy.   .....

    i Lucy learns how Miss Lavish discovered her secret.   .....

    j Lucy and George play tennis.   .....

After you read

17 How does Lucy feel, and why, after:

    a seeing George by the pool?

    b defending Cecil to her mother?

    c talking to her mother during dinner?

    d talking to Miss Bartlett in the sitting room?

    e talking to George and Mr Emerson after church?

    f playing tennis with George?

    g Cecil reads from *In a Piazza*?

    h talking to Miss Bartlett in her room?

    i George talks to her in the dining room?

    j talking to Cecil?

18 Discuss these questions.

    a How does George feel when Mrs Honeychurch introduces him
to Miss Bartlett after church? Why?

    b What is the difference between Cecil's and George's attitude to
women? Who do you agree with most? Why?

    c Is Lucy right to end her engagement with Cecil? Why (not)?

Chapters 13–15

Before you read

19 Discuss these questions with another student.

    a How will these people feel about the end of Lucy's engagement? Why?

    Mrs Honeychurch   Freddy   Mr Beebe   Miss Bartlett

    Mr Emerson

    b How do you think the story will end? Why?

While you read

20 Who

    a tells Mr Beebe about the end of Lucy's engagement? ....

    b approves of the end of the engagement? ....

    c is not as upset as she seems? ....

    d immediately approves of Lucy's desire to go to Greece? ....

    e does not believe in marriage? ....

    f does not want the end of Lucy's engagement to be a secret? ....

    g is Lucy becoming less close to? ....

    h believes in Truth and hates muddles? ....

    i secretly helps George and Lucy? ....

After you read

21 Think back to your answers to Question 19a. To what extent were you right?

22 Discuss how important these people are in this part of the story.

    a The Miss Alans

    b Mr Beebe

    c Mr Emerson

    d Miss Bartlett

23 Work with another student. Imagine that the two of you are going on holiday to Italy with three other people.

    a Which three people from the following list would you prefer to go with, and why?

      Miss Bartlett Mrs Honeychurch Cecil Mr Beebe Freddy Mr Emerson Miss Lavish

    b Would your three companions be happy in each other's company? Why (not)?

24 Discuss these questions.

    a What are the most famous novels about life in your country a hundred years ago?

    b Which ones have you read? Summarise the plot.

    c How are the lives and experiences of the main characters different from the lives of the people in *A Room with a View*?

Writing

25 'It was the old, old battle of the room with a view.' Explain the importance of the room with a view in this book.

26 Imagine that you are Sir Harry Otway (Chapter 7). Write a description of Cissie Villa for an advertisement in a property magazine. Describe the villa and the people in the neighbourhood. What kind of people are you looking for to rent it and why?

27 Imagine that you are Miss Bartlett (Chapter 12). Write a letter to Miss Lavish after your conversation with Lucy.

28 What do Lucy and George do between Chapters 14 and 15? Summarise this part of the story.

29 You are Mr Beebe's superior. What are Mr Beebe's strengths and weaknesses as a vicar? Should he be offered a more important job? Why (not)? Write a report on him.

30 Imagine that you are Lucy, in Venice with George. Write a letter to your mother, explaining why you have disobeyed her wishes and why she must accept George as her son-in-law.

31 What will happen when Lucy and George return to England? Write the next part of the story.

32 'Ladies were not inferior to men; they were different.' What have you learnt about the role of women in early twentieth-century England from this book?

33 'It might be possible to be nice to her; it was impossible to like her.' Describe the character of Charlotte Bartlett. How sympathetic are you towards her? Why?

34 Describe the Emersons and their relationship. Why do some of the people in the book disapprove of them? Are they right to disapprove of them? Why (not)?

WORD LIST

bachelor (n) an unmarried man

baptize (v) to make someone a member of the Christian church in a religious ceremony in which they are touched or covered with water

cab (n) a taxi

cad (n) a man whose behaviour is unprincipled and morally unacceptable

chaperone (n) a person who, in the past, went with a young unmarried woman to look after her and make sure that she behaved properly

clergyman (n) a male priest

conventional (adj) thinking and behaving in the normal way

despise (v) to strongly dislike someone

embrace (n/v) the act of putting your arms round someone and holding them in a loving way

exclaim (v) to say something suddenly and loudly because you are surprised, excited or angry

fate (n) a power that is believed to control what happens in people's lives; the things, usually bad or serious, that happen to someone

gratitude (n) the feeling of being grateful

maid (n) a female servant

muddle (n/v) a state of confusion, so that mistakes are made

murmur (v) to speak very softly and quietly

nude (adj) not wearing any clothes

outing (n) a short trip for a group of people

passion (n) a very strong feeling, usually of love or of belief in something

pension (n) a small hotel, especially in Italy, France or Spain

porter (n) someone whose job is to carry bags, in a hotel for example

respectable (adj) behaving in a way that people think is socially acceptable or morally right

sermon (n) a religious talk given in church

sigh (n/v) the act of breathing out heavily, especially when you are tired or annoyed

tactful (adj) careful not to say or do any thing that will upset or embarrass other people

tolerate (v) to accept or allow something, especially something that you dislike

tram (n) an electric vehicle for carrying passengers that moves along the street on metal tracks

vicar (n) a priest in the Church of England

villa (n) a house with a garden in the countryside or near the sea

violet (n) a small, sweet-smelling dark purple flower

wince (v) to tighten the muscles in your face because you have seen or remembered something embarrassing or unpleasant